♀MG – That Woman!

An anthology about women who perform miracles
and a few for whom a miracle was needed to stop them

Edited by

Lynne Gregg and Roger Paulding

Aakenbaaken & Kent　　　　　　　　**New York**

OMG – That Woman!

An anthology about women who perform miracles
and a few for whom a miracle was needed to stop them

Aakenbaaken & Kent   New York, NY 10003
akeditor@inbox.com

ISBN: 978-1-938436-12-3

TABLE OF CONTENTS

OMG – That Woman!

Our title happened by chance one day when a Houston Writers Guild critique group, one of several in the city and surrounding areas, was having lunch together. As writers, we're all storytellers, and someone told a hysterical story. Still laughing, another member added a funny comment, and the final remark was "OMG – that woman!" Our wise Guild president, Roger Paulding said, "That would make a great title for our next anthology." With smiling faces, everyone agreed. Roger continued, "But the stories have to be about strong women—not a bunch of love stories."

OMG – That Woman! has been fun for Guild members to write and for Roger and me to edit. We've laughed. We've cried. We've gasped. We've cringed, but it's *all* good.

Lynne Gregg

Get Me Some Tea

By Karleen Koen

A funny thing has happened on this journey I call my life.

I grew up watching women do all the household chores and hearing men, my grandfather Clyde in particular, call out from his domino game, "Woman, get me some tea." There was no respect for the domestic chores that kept our home cozy – the cleaning, the cooking, the errands – and I didn't respect them either.

Someone I cared about took a long time dying, and I had to help him out, literally and figuratively. He was a creative cook, and in his passing, he had a fussy palate. Somewhere in that, in his delight and interest in what I was doing, I began to see the creativity of a good cook and to find it fun, to find grace in serving what I had cooked to others. This sense of service, this sense of creativity, of ordering, has even spread to housework.

I have a new kinship with women I loved but whose work I didn't know I scorned: Mother, Aunt Eva, Nana, Aunt Lily, others. I think of them as I dust or vacuum – the way Aunt Eva made biscuits from scratch every single morning, how they sat doughy in the pan, and she would take a spoon and press an imprint of its fat bottom into each mound, then spoon some bacon grease in the resulting hollow before placing the pan in the oven, and the aroma of rising biscuits floated through the house and drew us into the kitchen. How Mother always kept our house neat and precise; how she sewed all of my clothes, including my wedding gown. I wonder what was in her mind as she pushed the soft, white fabric of that gown through the pulsing, mechanical needle of her sewing machine. Aunt Lily crocheted and made quilts and dollies, embroidered them all. I sleep on a pillowcase upon which her flowers swirl and cascade.

Until now I never saw their art: cooking, cleaning, sewing, keeping a family marching forward in cleanliness and with filled stomachs. A quiet art, the art of a good meal, the shine of a dusted table, the precise fullness of an embroidered flower. Ephemeral. Fleeting. Life.

Karleen Koen is the *New York Times* Best Selling author of *Through a Glass Darkly, Dark Angels, Now Face to Face,* and *Before Versailles, a Novel of Louis XIV.* She lives in Houston.

My Closet, Her Closet

Roger Paulding

Until recently, I was convinced I was spawned on Mars and dropped off on Chester Street in Stillwater, Oklahoma because no one in the galaxy would have me. I muddled through childhood, certain that I was adopted, never mind being the spitting image of every male in the family who preceded me, especially my Dad Leo. Only in the last year of my mother's life did I discover that I was indeed her child.

The things about me that I considered eccentric with regard to my family— my love of good music, my passion for reading, my affection for words, my enthusiasm for politics—were traits which Mom hid in a private closet.

Well, not the political stuff, she was very vocal about that. On that, we seldom saw eye to eye. She telephoned me at six a.m. to inform me with delight that Ike had beaten Adlai.

Mom played the part of a ditsy blonde most of her life. She knew a smart woman did not upstage her school-teacher husband, my father. Her favorite saying was, "When God passed out brains, I thought he said pains, and I said, 'No thanks, I don't want any.'" We believed her. Nearly to the day she departed.

When Dad died, I moved back home so she would not be alone. I was sixty-four and still the single son. When a storm cut off the television along with the rest of the electrical power, she and I were forced to listen to a battery-powered radio. I finagled the dial until I found NPR. They were discussing the components of an orchestra, playing several bars on an instrument and giving the listener a moment to identify it before they corrected errors. Without a single mistake, Mom recognized each instrument as the bars filtered through the tiny boom box. It was my first hint that she owned a closet. She was not the woman we thought she was, nothing like the blonde in the ubiquitous jokes.

Fast forward to 2008 when I became her primary caregiver, soon after she celebrated her ninety-fifth birthday. Each morning, relying on a walker for locomotion, she came into the den for breakfast and a turn at CNN. Her spirit was indomitable. She seldom failed to greet me with a song. "Good morning to you, good morning to you. We're all in our places with sunshiny faces. Oh, this is the way to start a new day!"

Not a tune carrier—I had been damaged in fourth grade music class when the girl in front of me blurted, "Roger can't carry the tune!"—nevertheless I sang along with Mom.

"Good Morning to You" became our song. Later, when she was bedfast and frequently anxious she would not make the five steps to the bathroom without falling, I entreated her, "Let's sing our song." And she belted it out as she trooped into the facility, although now and then, I sang alone. And when a caregiver located an old hymnal, this nonbeliever joined Mom and we sang "Jesus Loves Me" and "I Come to the Garden Alone." Mom never complained that I was off-key.

If I never let Mom know I was agnostic, neither did I tell her about my sexual orientation. My grandmother sent Mom a letter while I was in college in which she wrote—rather matter-of-factly—that she hoped I would grow out of falling in love with boys. Mom glossed over such revelations or pretended she had no acquaintance with such matters, but through the years, she offered support when my liaisons fell apart. Dad, however, made a habit of homophobic comments in my presence. Once he said of a TV news anchor, "I don't like him. He looks gay."

After Dad's death, I debated telling Mom about myself. I feared the admission would result in a train wreck. A few days before she died, in a tactful manner, she tried to open the door to my closet.

"Did you say you were gay?"

I kept the door closed. Coward that I was, I wanted it to remain a secret.

Most of my life, I shunned being the stereotypical homosexual male who doted on his mother. I discussed her briefly with friends and acquaintances. Frequently, I frowned and squelched the subject if someone asked, "How's your Mom?" I thought the question snide, that they had figured out my secret and wanted me to be aware. Maybe they had. Who knows?

Mom had other things in her closet, too. When I was nineteen, rummaging through a China closet for some napkins, I found the Marriage Certificate. She and Dad had not married September 25 1929, as we had been told, but rather in November. I was born the following June. For more than fifty years, my sister, my brothers, and I never revealed what we knew. She was a good Baptist and a good mother, and she was entitled.

Mom remained a glamorous lady until the end of her days, perhaps a little vain, but able to put the Gabor women to shame. I loved to tell her she was the most beautiful mother I had. She understood I would say anything to produce a laugh, and she would come back with, "How many mothers do you have?" or if she felt a little under the weather, "The rest of them must not look like much."

And she was in full possession of her faculties. She did as much around the house as I did. In her nineties, she lost interest in cooking, and her financial affairs, following an overdose of anesthesia. She still loved to discuss politics, and to read, although glaucoma put an end to that endeavor. When she reached her last year, she had forgotten many things, but her mind was sharp. She stayed close to her bed, unsure whether she was in the hospital or a rest home. She loved to hear stories about her early life. I reminded her that she was seventeen when I was born. I asked if she recalled Dr. Waggoner and did she remember that he came to the house on Chester Street to deliver me. She responded, "No one ever told me about that."

Last spring, I took her to a new doctor who prefaced an introduction to me with the statement, "You've got to put your mother in a rest home." I cried all the way back home. *Never.* I would never do that. And I never did. How grateful I am for that decision. It was mostly during the last months that I came to know her. Frequently, I slept in the recliner in her bedroom. We had outside caregivers for many hours, sometimes all night, so I could catch up on my sleep. The important thing was that she remained at home in her own room, in the bed she and Dad had shared.

I became the caregiver 24/7, feeding her, lying beside her at night when she thought she was abandoned, helping her to and from the bathroom and all the necessities that entailed. No son ever wants to see a parent naked, but such reluctances fade into the ether when alone without female help. Once, as she sat naked on the bed while I tried to extract paper undies from the package, she asked, "No one is going to take advantage of me, are they?"

Mom was not always certain who I was. Sometimes, she thought I was Leo, the love of her life, a Ron and Nancy sort of thing, eyes only for each other. After all, in her final days, when she called for Leo, I was the one who showed up. Other times she wasn't sure that I wasn't a stranger who had wandered into the wrong house. My reward came when my often-absent sister did something Mom appreciated and then asked, "Do you know who I am?"

Mom answered, "Yes, you're Roger."

Although I refused to open my closet, I was grateful that Mom opened hers and revealed herself. In early February, hammered by a stroke as she sat on the edge of the bed, instinctively, she turned and lay down, already in the clutches of death. I leaned into her ear and told her I loved her. From her pillow, she managed her final, barely comprehensible words: "I love you, too."

Roger Paulding is the author of *Bought Off* and *The Pickled Dog Caper.* He is the founder of the Houston Writers Guild.

Love's Boiling Point

A strangely assertive woman takes a cop home for dinner

Chris Rogers

The thousand charms of Adin Carp I resisted as best I could, but when he touched me, even that most casual of touches, I knew I was lost. Some, who know the nature of my soul, claim I am a creature of passion, that I love too deeply. Passion is superficial, at best. From Adin, I wanted that invasive, soul-wrenching love that bridges all differences.

For though I look like other women—walk, talk, dress and even smell like other women—there remains a difference. It was important that Adin know me for myself before we surrendered to the passion that inflamed us both.

It should be understood that neither by word nor gesture had I given Adin a hint that I would succumb to his charms. I continued, as always, to deflect his advances with a bright smile and a clever come-back; he could not guess the willpower required for such restraint.

Adin's weakness—although in other regards he was a man of disciplined habits—bordered on obsession: he loved fine food. He prided himself on his gourmet palate. In this respect I do not differ materially. I take pride in my culinary skills and indulge my epicurean appetites.

About dusk one evening during the hottest weeks of the Galveston summer, I caught up with Adin at a happy-hour bar on The Strand. He greeted me with excessive delight, for he had been drinking. The man looked splendid. He wore snug white shorts and shirt, accentuating his handsome physique, his dusky tan. Sun-kissed brown hair had grown curly with the damp sea air, and his blue eyes shone from the effects of the excellent wine he offered me. I was so pleased to see him I had to sit down at once to steady my pulse.

"We found the body on the beach," Adin was saying to his blonde female companion. Adin worked for Galveston Homicide Division. Apparently, I had interrupted a morbid police story. "Not an ounce of fluid or tissue left in it, just rubbery skin over dry bones."

"How lucky I am to bump into you tonight," I said.

"Second body this month, same weird condition—"

"A friend sent me a pair of New Brunswick lobsters," I interjected firmly. "The finest. But—broil alive or boil alive? I cannot decide."

"Lobsters?" His eyes brightened. "New Brunswick? And in the middle of summer!"

"I cannot decide," I repeated. "They are huge. I was silly enough to hope you might join me for dinner. When I could not find you, and now that I see you are already with company—"

Adin's pert blonde friend glared in my direction.

"Perhaps I should ask Fred Larkin," I said.

"Larkin?"

"Huge. You would have to see to believe."

"But Larkin? He's a poultry man."

"Huge—and at their prime."

"New Brunswick lobsters …"

"Since you are already engaged, I should look up Fred. If anyone has a dependable appetite, it is he. He will tell me—"

"Larkin doesn't know a lobster from a clam."

"And yet some say there is not a dish he has not mastered."

"Let's go." He bid a brusque goodbye to the blonde, then waved the waiter over and paid for another bottle of the excellent chardonnay to take with us. He uncorked the wine on the spot. "To sharpen our palates."

"My lodgings are west of the docks," I said, accepting a plastic tumbler half filled. "It is a fine night for a walk."

"But too hot for that dress you're wearing." He thumbed a bead of sweat from my lip.

I shivered at his touch.

We strolled away from the bar, and in the waning sunlight his eyes looked dark and sensual.

"Surely you have a swim suit under that dress. Take off the top, at least." In one smooth, quick motion, he flicked open my buttons.

I gasped. My breasts strained for his fingers.

But I reined in my passion. The night was young, and my plans for Adin included a long, slow ascension to love's boiling point. With a shift of my shoulders, the blouse slid down to my waist, where I tied the tails in a quick knot.

"Now yours," I said.

He smiled, setting the bottle down on a piling, his glass alongside. His shirt came off as quickly as mine. He tucked it through his belt, magnificent shoulders glistening with dampness. My mouth went suddenly dry.

His eyes dipped into my cleavage. "You're a chesty little broad, aren't you?"

"So I have been told."

Night fell as we walked. We came at length to the west pier and stood together looking at the docking lights reflected in the water. We had finished half the wine. Adin's speech had begun to slur.

"Another dollop?" He pretended to miss my tumbler, splashing my chest with the chilly liquid. "Oops! Sorry. I'll fix it."

Stepping close, he dipped his head to the swell of flesh above my swim top. His tongue glided over my skin, scooping up the droplets of wine and leaving a burning trail in its wake. It was all I could do to resist clutching him nearer. I held my arms rigidly at my sides.

"My place is just up the way," I said evenly.

His lips brushed the base of my throat, my cheek, the corner of my mouth. Summoning an image of the Arctic cap to cool my scalding blood, I managed barely to remain still. He looked in my eyes, and I could see the love beginning to shine in his.

"Lobsters?" he murmured, at length.

"Lobsters," I replied, then glanced down. "Have your shorts always been so tight?"

He grinned. "Only on occasion."

It took a moment for my poor Adin to relax enough to resume our walk.

"Maybe we should have an appetizer before dinner," he suggested at last, his eyes roving over my body.

"And spoil the lobsters? Perhaps I should call Larkin, after all. You may not consider the catch choice enough for your superior palate. Shall we stop at this ice house and see if someone will drive you back to your blonde friend?"

"Enough," he said. "Broiled alive. With a dressing of lemon and honey and drawn butter that will make you forget Larkin ever existed."

I kicked off my sandals. "The quickest way to get there is to swim."

"In our clothes?"

"We can leave them here." I showed him my cache, tucked under the pier, a plastic case with a tight seal.

In seconds, our outer garments and shoes were stashed. As his gaze washed over my bare haunches in the thong bikini, the front of his Spandex trunks bulged in appreciation.

He moved toward me. My breath caught in my chest, hot as an August drought. I hungered for him.

Turning quickly, I dove into the tepid water, imagining I heard a faint sizzle as the liquid touched my flushed skin. The soothing sea enveloped me, awakening memories. It slithered up my legs and beneath my suit, swirling, stroking.

Frantic to work off the carnal urges, I streaked through the water like an eel, glancing back only once to assure myself that Adin was close behind. We came to the boat. I broke the surface, spied the rope ladder in the moonlight, and waited for my lover to bob up beside me.

He sluiced his hair back with one hand and reached for me with the other.

"I want you," he said.

"The invitation was for dinner."

"Then I want you for dessert."

I flashed my most inscrutable smile and started up the ladder. He climbed close behind, his breath hot on my buttocks.

I climbed faster. Dropping to the deck, I shivered in the night air.

"I've seen this boat," Adin said, looking around as he boarded. "It's a derelict."

"Perfect for a recluse like me."

"But what gives? You just move aboard, set up housekeeping?" I could hear his policeman's curiosity champing behind the question.

"I like it here, the ocean lapping at my walls, rocking me to sleep at night."

Below deck, I watched him get a sense of my world. I had transformed the living area with shimmering paint and cushiony leather furnishings set in deep recesses in the bulkhead. The space glistened like an underworld fantasy, all green and glossy in the subdued light, with bits of bright color like darting fish. Photographs of exquisite sea creatures dotted the walls. My own portrait hung above the couch.

The salty sea air, heavy with humidity, slid along our skin and filled our nostrils.

"We'll want to rinse off," I said. "Before we get itchy." I pointed to the tiny head, with its inclusive shower. "You first, if you like."

He stood close. The heat from our skin mingled and rose between us like steam, smelling of salt and musk and need.

"What about that appetizer?" he coaxed.

"I will make a salad and pour us another glass of wine," I said firmly. The night was still young. I would not embrace my lover until he fully understood me.

"The lobsters?" he said.

I uncovered the tank. The two monsters lazed in icy water.

"They're incredible! But we can't possibly eat them both."

"Perhaps you underestimate our appetites." I smiled and shooed him toward the shower, then made the salad as promised, crisp and green and spicy. It was important to me that Adin's gourmet appetite be satisfied before my own.

By the time we finished eating, the moon, visible through the porthole, hung in the midnight sky like a plump yellow melon. Adin had polished off the better part of both lobsters by himself, their meat sweet and tender. Watching him enjoy the food only heightened my own pleasure. My head swam from the wine, my lips felt slick and sweet with the drawn butter sauce. My eyes feasted on Adin's gorgeous body.

"Ready for dessert?" he whispered, seeing the flush of my skin, the feverish desire in my eyes.

"There is something I have to tell you first."

"Oh, God, spare me the true confessions. Believe me, I've heard them all."

"Not this one," I said. "Not from me."

"You've led a scarlet life," he suggested. "You've used men, or been used by men, or you've never had a man in your life and fear you might be frigid. You were fondled by your father—or your mother, or both. You have a fetish for men's jock straps, or a fondness for being spanked. Whatever it is, I don't want to hear it unless it affects what we're going to do right this minute. The past is past. The future can take care of itself. I want you *now*, damn it."

He reached across the table and took my hand. I did not pull away. It was time. Blood rushed to my loins and throat and head, making me dizzy with wanting him. My breath came in short, quick sips.

"I am different," I said.

He stood and pulled me toward him, urging me to the leather couch.

"You sure are, and I like it." His quick fingers unhooked my swim top. It dropped away, my heavy breasts spilling forward.

"This is not the real me," I whispered. "I am not of the Earth." My voice sounded thick and raspy.

He grinned, sliding his fingers into the elastic of my bikini bottoms. "So you're a mermaid, or maybe a sea urchin. I can handle that."

I seized his clever fingers and held them still. My head pounded with hunger for him. My temperature soared, though I struggled to control it.

"The place I come from is much like your sea," I said, "but it is not on this world." Sweat poured down my sides, down my arms and into my palms, loosening my hold on his fingers.

"Jeez, you're burning up." He pulled his hands free. "Are you sick?"

"I am in love."

"In heat is more like it." His hand felt cool against my forehead. "Well, come on. Let's stop talking and give you what you're panting for."

He squeezed my breasts gently. My head began to spin.

"The photograph," I gasped. "The portrait above the couch …" My bikini had disappeared, along with his trunks. I felt the thrust of him against my belly. I pushed away. "You have to look at the photograph."

"Yeah, okay. I see it. Some kind of squid thing."

Cupping my bottom in his wide hands, he started to lower me to the couch. I tried to resist, but my blood had reached the simmer point. It was too late— far too late.

"Tell me you like it," I rasped. We sank to the couch, the buttery soft leather enfolding us. "Tell me it is beautiful."

"Sure," he said, spreading my legs. "If you like squid, I guess it's a beautiful picture." His cool hardness invaded me. "God, you're like a furnace."

Or a pressure cooker. My blood had reached the boiling point. My mouth closed over Adin's as I gave in completely to his charms. I wrapped my arms around him, then my legs, my arms, my legs, my arms, my legs.

His screams of pleasure raced through my head as I loved him, tasted him. His fluids mixed with mine, pumping through my veins as mine pumped through his, boiling, boiling, the tissues liquefying. Our very souls throbbed with heat and love and joy.

Chris Rogers has taught mystery writing at Rice University School of Continuing Studies, The University of Houston, the Women's Institute of

Houston and in private master writing classes. Her students have received numerous awards and acknowledgements. As a ghostwriter, she helps authors craft nonfiction books, articles and essays. After a career in graphic design, Chris became a writer, and subsequently became one of the most beloved teachers of writing in the Houston area.

Caveat

Roger Paulding

That woman gets what she wants or she does without.

I pegged her right off, unsure if she considered me qualified until that red hair flashed and she pointed a pink fingernail at me.

"Don't go away. I think I want you."

Flattered, I couldn't help hitching up my jeans and giving her my best grin.

She glanced at the piece of paper in her hand. "Jake—how do you say that?"

"Pah-troos-key."

"You speak Spanish?"

"Comme ci, comme ça."

The beautiful redhead made her way around the room, speaking to just about everyone. She tapped three men and pointed them toward the front door. Then she came back to me.

"Get your gear and meet me at the yellow beast." All business. "Only one in the parking lot. You won't have any trouble finding it."

"Hold on. Mind telling me why you want me?"

"Gut instinct. Always go by my gut instinct."

"And the work involves what?"

"Sheep ranch. Lazy B. Fifty miles north of here."

I could tell by the way she talked that she was unsure of herself. Maybe she didn't trust that gut instinct one hundred percent.

"And your name is?"

"Alicia Baker. The big enchilada. You keep me happy, you got yourself a steady job."

This could be interesting. When I walked into the Topeka employment office that morning, my chances of getting hired seemed remote. Twenty experienced-looking forty-something guys with their thumbs in their back pockets were looking for work. I was not too excited about being picked. It was October, long past lambing and shearing season, a time a rancher could do without extra hired hands if he or she so wanted. Maybe do without a foreman, if she knew how to deal the cards.

"Lazy B is a profitable enterprise," Alicia went on. "I intend to keep it that way. My Dad died last year. Family said I couldn't manage the ranch. Proved them wrong, so far. Do you think you can hold up your end of the blanket?"

"Without a doubt."

I had never worked for a lady boss before. She could not have been very experienced—a year younger than me, maybe a year older—just for your information, I'm still considered college material by certain misguided souls.

"You got yourself a hard worker," I added, with a big grin. The grin didn't faze her. First woman I ever met who wasn't fazed by it. Mom always said, lucky would be the woman who woke up every morning to that grin of mine. So far, I hadn't found one disposed to suffer that delight more than once or twice, although there was nothing wrong with what went with that grin. I hitched up my jeans again, hoping it didn't look like I was preening.

Once I and the others belted ourselves in the Hummer, Alicia twisted the key, listened for the motor to turn over and then announced, "This is your foreman, gentlemen. Get used to it."

I looked at the three leathery-skinned gents who sat behind me and wondered which one she meant. She clapped her hand on my shoulder and I realized I was the designated honcho. The two older guys grunted without comment. The other so flustered, I had a feeling he wanted to say something about me being wet behind the ears. But he clamped his lips shut and pulled out a cigarette. Then he went for his lighter, thought better of it, and stashed the cigarette behind his ear.

At five o'clock, Alicia fired the frustrated smoker and cashiered him out. After that, one of the others relied on Spearmint and took precise care to call me *sir* and her *ma'am*. Old-fashioned in my book, but I'm not a complainer.

"Sometimes, I make a mistake," Alicia whispered to me as the discharged one grabbed his duffle and headed for the door. She didn't drive him back to town. Another hired hand showed up from out back and took him away in an old Dodge truck.

"Last meal of the day is at six," Alicia announced. She looked me over like I was a prize she had found in a *Cracker Jack* box. "After that, Jake, you and the hired hands can set out for the bunkhouse on the north forty. Attached to the sheep barn. You get the private room. The crew sleeps dorm style. Showers and toilets are communal. Here's the key to your room. You may want to lock it at night so one of your friends doesn't sneak in and light a match between your toes."

"I'll take my chances," I said.

She tossed the keys in my direction. With my right hand, I snatched them mid-air. She gave me a weird grin, evidently pleased with my dexterity. If that were a test of my sexual orientation, I pretended I didn't understand. *Brokeback Mountain* and all that.

"You got a cell phone?" she asked. "In case I want to talk to you while you're riding the rim? You do know how to ride, don't you?"

"Sure do." I looked away, slightly embarrassed, pretending she didn't understand the ambiguity of those words.

By the end of October, I entertained second thoughts about the job. Not easy working all day next to a gorgeous babe that you know is off-limits. Once in a while, I caught her giving me a long look, but then she quickly looked away.

Her modus operandi was don't mess around with the hired help. Six weeks of fantasizing about Alicia were all I intended to subject my libido to. I thought about moving on, maybe south to Texas where winters aren't as severe as Kansas. And where the male ranch owners are downright ugly and walk bowlegged.

Couple nights later, Alicia asked me to check the south rim, make sure the fences were in good order and the sheep had found their way into the fold. Midnight, on my return, when I rode by the stock tank, I glimpsed her sitting on a little hill chucking stones into the water, the newly formed ice crackling with each toss.

Sort of thing I did when I was a kid if things turned south for me. Her problems weren't any of my business, so I kept riding, keeping an eye on the steely sky. The temp hovered around twenty and my nose grew stiff in the ripening cold. The next morning, a snowstorm roared in like an angry polar bear. Visibility was still viable but not something you could count on. Alicia oversaw the herding of the sheep into the barn, counted them and told me three had gone missing. Could I ride out and find them before the mercury dived lower?

"Yeah, sure," I said, and almost added, by the way, this is my last week. Something in her green eyes stopped me. Something had hurt her. Sure enough, I opened my big mouth about having seen her last night. Told her that I did the same thing as a boy when my world caved in.

"Letter from my fiancé came yesterday. Gone to France for a year." There came a glint of understanding in her eyes—but only for a moment—then they turned cold. "Wants to find himself—or someone else—the asshole. We were going to be married in December."

Well, fancy words aren't my forte. Didn't need them. Before I could open my mouth, she continued, "You'd better get on trusty old Dusty and find those wayward sheep before they turn into frozen lamp chops."

"Rusty," I said. "Was told the horse is named Rusty."

"Oh, yeah. Dusty old Rusty."

I gave her the grin. "Dusty's sort of on the rusty side, too."

Right away, I wish I hadn't said it, but she didn't catch on.

Anyway, I decided not to volunteer that I wouldn't think of abandoning the fort when the Indians were climbing the ladder. Not my nature to leave when someone's in trouble, but some things are better left unsaid. I wrestled on my sheepskin jacket and headed out into the winter gloom. The snowstorm whirled and cut at Rusty and me, somehow or other getting between the saddle and my balls. There wasn't a square millimeter of me not in danger of frost bite. Rusty wasn't happy with me, and chattered his displeasure most of the way to the back forty. You didn't have to be a horse whisperer to understand his complaints. When I explained to him that we had a job to do, he seemed to feel better.

We were a good distance from the barn when I heard a sheep bleat. Barely heard her over the windstorm, but sounded like she was in trouble. I halted Rusty, got down and tramped through deep snow, icicles forming on my eyelashes. I found an aging dam beside a lean-to that held a few bales of hay. She was circling the frozen ground, sniffing at the dead grass, looking for a place to drop a newborn. Way out of season. She was so fat, no one had realized she was preggers.

I grabbed some hay from one of the bales and distributed it on the ground to make a pallet. The ewe slipped to her side, nervous, straining and not too thrilled. I grabbed the blanket under Rusty's saddle and covered her with it. Then I punched the numbers into the cell phone for Alicia and went back to soothing the ewe. Headlights barely pierced the heavy white veil stretching down the sky when the Hummer busted over the horizon twenty minutes later.

"What have we got here?" Alicia asked as she stepped from the vehicle. "A damsel in distress?"

"You got supplies in the Hummer?"

"Some."

"Need a pair of Latex gloves. Antiseptic. Antibiotics. And towels."

"Stuff in the back. Dad kept a lot of things there for various uses. Don't know what all. He never taught me anything. Sent me to Juilliard when I was twelve."

Alicia knelt beside the ewe, her hands starting toward the animal.

"Uh-uh," I said. "Move back and don't touch her. Women are harmed by certain bacteria during lamb birth."

"You're making that up right?"

"Wrong. Sheep sometimes are infected with psittacosis and it's transmitted to women as lupus. That is, if you're pregnant."

She backed off with a quickly mumbled, "No way."

I pulled on the gloves, tested the antiseptic spray to make sure it worked. Down on my knees, I raised the ewe's tail and clipped tangled wool. Then I scrubbed the dam with Aloe Vesta. Smeared some on myself, coated my hands and arms with KY, and squirted some into the birth canal.

There was nothing other than admiration in Alicia's gator-green eyes. "Should I be calling you *Doctor* Jake?"

"Not yet. Probably not ever, way things are going. "

Waiting was the prescribed treatment at this point. Patience. I whistled a little tune while the storm made its own music. Alicia danced around to keep warm. The mama sheep made noises, mostly whimpers.

Several minutes later, the water bag emerged, followed by the lamb's nose and a single hoof, but I needed two front legs. I pulled gently on the lamb's head and the other foot appeared. When the lamb was free of the birth canal, the mama ewe licked its face. The little tyke strained to get up, fell back. Mama kept cleaning him. Minute by minute, the baby became more alert. At last, he struggled to his feet.

Alicia was impressed. "Now, can I call you doctor?"

I pulled off my gloves. "I'll have to think about it." I didn't say anything further.

Her face glistened with esteem. "You seem to know what you're doing."

"Couple of years at vet school," I explained. "Money ran out. Maybe I can go back next year. That stuff was on my resume."

"Damn. Forgot to read the resumes. But school's not the reason you're wanting to leave soon, is it?"

"How did you know I was considering that?"

"Gut instinct. About all I got going for me. I'll make you a promise. If you hang around, come February, maybe we can work spring semester into your spare time."

I injected a smidgen of sarcasm. "Like I get a lot of spare time. When would I study?"

"You got your Saturday nights free."

That toss of her red hair was meant to convince me and it worked. "Oh, yeah. So I do."

"You can use them to study. Or now and then, you might take me to a dance at the local honky-tonk." She cocked her head to the right. "You can dance, can't you?"

The big grin. "I can tangle—er—tango with the best of them."

"Awesome."

"Except I am a little rusty."

The sparkle in her eyes was positively shameless, but with a shy smile, she uttered a slight caveat. "Don't get too excited. Dusty may be rusty, but he stays in the saddle until we know each other better."

What's in a Name?

Sandra M. DiGiovanni

My mom named me after vomit. Yeah, you read that right. Vomit, as in barf, puke, throw-up. You're probably thinking I have the meanest, worst mom in the world. No so. Mom's the best. She's just a little left of center.

My name is Tsunami Cloud Adams. Mom said she had morning sickness so bad, that when she threw up, it looked like a tsunami in the toilet bowl when she flushed. Did I tell you my mom was a hippie? She calls herself a flower child. I say hippie. She liked the sound of the word tsunami. She still says it's a winding word, like a gold bracelet on Cleopatra's arm. I asked why she didn't call me Cleo. She gave me the fisheye as if to ask what planet I'm from.

Mom doesn't get it when I say I was named after vomit. I mean, she gets the tie-in from my point of view, but she does-not-get-it. I want to change my name. The first time I brought up the name change, she went into a blue funk for a month. She walked around all sad, like somebody peed in her Cheerios. I was ten, for crying out loud. I wanted a name like Shelby or Savannah or Ashley. Now that I'm fifteen, I realize those names wouldn't suit me. I'm more like a Zena, ya know?

My middle name, Cloud, came from when Mom gave birth. I was born in a commune in Oregon. Yes, communes still exist. Anyway, Mom wanted to give birth outdoors in water. The closest water outside was the public swimming pool a mile away or the rushing river about fifty yards away. For some reason, both choices were disregarded. Go figure. My dad came up with the idea of a kiddie pool. My mom said they were cheap and that she didn't think the sides would hold up when she leaned on them. Dad dug a hole and put the pool in it. Mom had him fill it with water, tried it out, and loved it. They kept the pool inside for sanitary purposes, and Dad kept the hole in the ground ready. He had to watch the stupid dog next door, though. That dumb poodle used the hole to do his business every day. One day while Dad was cleaning poop from the hole, our neighbor, the dog's owner, hollered to see what Dad was doing. Dad saluted him and told him to keep his damned dog in their cabin area. Dad's eyes glazed over as he realized that putting a birthing pool in the front yard was probably a bad idea. The area behind the cabin was a little more private since our three room house was L-shaped, so Dad dug a new hole there.

My mom's water broke at high noon that mid-July day while she was talking to old Mr. Castle, our neighbor from across the street. Mom had gotten some of his mail by mistake and was taking it to him when he was coming down his path to check his. They chatted by his mailbox when *sploosh*, water gushed from between my mom's legs under her long broom skirt. Mr. Castle was a single gentleman who'd never married. Imagine his surprise when his neighbor splashed him with amniotic fluid.

My mom is what some people might consider an "earth mother." She is all about natural. She wanted a natural birth, breastfeeding, no Dacron or rayon or nylon. She baked her own bread. She'd milk a cow if there was one nearby.

Mom had been having twinges since daybreak, but she dismissed them as nuisance pains. Mom blithely went about her daily activities till her first serious contraction came about half an hour after the big splash. (By the way, I filched all this birth info from Mom's journals. She is a prodigious writer.) Mom bent over in half when the first contraction hit. She dropped the towel she was hanging on the line. I think she was surprised that it *hurt*. Well, what did she expect? She'd be squeezing a watermelon out of an opening the size of a grapefruit.

She immediately shuffled to the carpentry shop where Dad shared his time with other commune folk. He was about to finish a chair and go take his turn in the community garden. That night no turnip greens filled anyone's pots. Halfway back to their cabin, Mom had another contraction. She drew blood on Dad's forearm and cursed a blue streak. Able Jones stuck his head out a window and laughed, telling Dad he was in for a wild ride. Mom marched over to Able, insulted his mother, and screamed for his wife Sunflower. (Yeah, I know, but that is her *real* name.)

Sunny followed Mom and stopped her by the little rock garden in our yard. Pulling up mom's skirt and telling her to spread 'em, she looked and told Mom she had a little while to go yet. (Mom went commando in those days.) Mom then insulted Sunny's mom and said to call a doctor. Sunny took Mom inside and calmed her down. Dad stood in the middle of the road and looked foolish.

The third contraction hit mom in her butt and travelled down the back of her legs. She spit out the concoction that Sunny was giving her to ease the pain. Unfortunately Sunny was right in front of her. While our neighbor wiped herself off, Mom had another pain, less than a minute later. According to her journal, she uttered that word—you know, the "D" word—"Drugs!"

Mom was so ticked off about the pain. She had helped Sunny give birth to Solange the year before, and Sunny had had no pain. When Mom voiced this thought, Sunny sat down in the rattan-seated ladder-back chair and howled, tears of laughter streaming down her brown face. That somewhat aroused my mom's ire more.

"What's so flippin' funny?" Mom bellowed.

"I'd been in labor fourteen hours when you came over. I was too tired to do more than pant by the time you came over to help, Flare. You haven't been in labor all that long. Just you wait," Sunny sneered.

Flare, pretty name, right? It's a *hippie* name! Mom's real name is Mary Sue. When she and Dad moved to the commune, he said that her red-gold hair looked like a solar flare. The commune called her Flare after that. I don't get it. Dad's name is Jim.

I'm the oldest kid. After I was born, the folks did a very unhippie thing: they got married. Granted, it was a hippie ceremony, but they are legally wed. Only married folks in the commune. Some things I do not understand.

Anyway back to Mom's labor. Dad had filled the kiddie pool a little past half full. Hot water would fill the rest. Neighbors on both sides had pots of water on simmer. Dad had a cauldron of water heating over the fire a little behind the house. Mom was still in the house trying to sip cactus juice and whatever else was in Sunny's brew. Mom seemed to think that wasn't up to par with a saddle block. With no air conditioning and open windows, Mom's forum was quite public.

Sunny took Mom to the bedroom and helped her strip and lie on the bed. Our little midwife took a gander at Australia, ya know, the land down under, and gurgled in surprise. "Why, Flare, you're almost fully dilated. You stay here and relax. Whatever you do, don't start pushing. You haven't been in labor much over an hour. How....?" Shaking her head, she hurried out to get the hot water added to the kiddie pool.

Dad and Sunny spread a canvas tarp beside the pool so they would stay clean. Sunny gathered the prepared birthing supplies, and Dad stood there with his big hands dangling by his khaki seams. Inside the house, Mom roared, and our neighbor hied hence to Mantua (the bedroom). Mom was pacing the bedroom, trailing pink water on the green and white tiles.

"Another contraction? Need to push?" questioned Sunflower.

"No contractions. Can I change my mind about this?" Mom asked.

"Well, yeah, we can go to the hospital," Sunny answered.

"No! I mean, do I hafta do this *now*?" Mom said.

"Do *what* now?"

"This thing in my stomach! Do I hafta do this now?" Mom demanded.

"You don't have a choice," Sunshine laughed. "Tell me when you're about to have another contraction so we can breathe."

"*You* breathe. I'm going out to sit in the pool," Mom snapped, and out the door she went, naked as a jaybird.

Mom stepped into the pool and sat. Dad and Sunny sat on the tarp. Mom said, "Unth," and out I popped. Dad snapped to and climbed into the pool with Mom, Jesus sandals and all, scooping my little head out of the water and into the air. Dad said I hit the air howling like a coyote. All the birthing procedures occurred in the proper order as Mom held me to her breast where I apparently latched on like a professional.

I scarfed colostrum while Dad counted my toes. "Little Tsunami," he cooed. "Honey, she needs a middle name."

"Cloud," Mom stated. "See that cloud right over the pine tree? Looks like elephants mating? Some Native American women name their babies for the first thing they see after giving birth. I see a cloud of two elephants. Tsunami Cloud Adams." And here I am. I guess I should be grateful not to be Tsunami Two-Elephants-Mating Adams.

I was born ninety-seven minutes after Mom's water broke. I was the second longest labor. My littlest sister took over two hours. Mom had the others less than ninety minutes after the onset of labor, with the average number of contractions per labor, six. The doctors said Mom was built for birthing and that she was definitely not normal in that department. Duh.

I sneaked into all of Mom's journals to see how we got our names. Here we are, in birth order. Me. My sister Songbird Rhee. Songbird, because Mom heard a songbird as she gave birth in the bathtub. (Winter baby, doncha know?) Rhee, because that sounded like what the bird was singing. Where'd a winter songbird come from? That's what I'd like to know. Anyhow, we call her Birdy.

My second sister Rainbow Jolly. Mom was out in the kiddie pool again right after a rain. The rainbow was a full arc when Rainy came out, laughing. Both Mom and Dad swear to this, hence the middle name Jolly.

My brother Chuck Distant. Kiddie pool, midday. Mom saw a woodchuck off in the distance. So why not Woodchuck instead of plain Chuck? Mom said that would be wrong! Say what?

Then my baby sister, the "oops" baby. (Chucky was nine, and my parents thought they were finished.) In the claw footed bathtub, another winter baby. Mom slept through the birth. She chose this stage in her life to begin identifying with The Establishment, ya know, as in "Up the Establishment"? Baby sister "oops" got a normal name, well sort of.

Cheryl-Ann Celeste Adams. Awww, c'mon, do I have to spell it out?

Sandra M. DiGiovanni is a retired English and theater teacher living and writing in Sugar Land, Texas. When she's not writing, this lively grandma helps tutor her homeschooled grandsons, Bryce and Declan. In Sandra's bag of tricks are one and a half novels of women's fiction and tons of short stories. Her genesis in writing began with poetry in junior high and still continues. She has been published in one short story anthology and two poetry anthologies.

Death by Cancer—Death by Pills

Lynne C. Gregg

Brian died of lung cancer. His beautiful, blond wife of four years, Marny, seemed still, but her mind was racing as she plotted the end of her own life. She was intent on distancing herself from the world. Intent on finding a way to snuff out the tiny candle that was left burning in her heart. Intent on wiping away the memories of her lover's demise. Forever.

Brian had been a loyal friend and a handsome athlete. He was a successful entrepreneur who came home each day to become a simply perfect husband and lover. Marny could not imagine her life without him. Marny saw no reason to live without him.

At first, Marny tried to voice her opinion to Brian's mother. "Viewings are morbid. I know Brian wanted to be cremated. I don't want him rotting in a plot of earth."

"*You're* being morbid, Marny. Brian is my only child, and I don't want him burned. He *will* have a beautiful, normal funeral." Marny had no strength left to battle Brian's mother so she let her take over everything.

Whatever Brian's mother wanted, Marny agreed. "You choose the casket and the clothes Brian will wear. I can't do it." Brian's mother called it a celebration of his life. Marny wasn't celebrating.

The young widow stood tall and accepted condolences throughout the entire funeral while planning her own death. She thought of her options. *I could shoot myself, but where would I get a gun? I could hang myself, but how and where? I could overdose on pills since I have plenty of painkillers left over from Brian.* Pills seemed the best possibility, so far.

At the crowded funeral home, Marny didn't see the flowers for Brian lining every wall. She didn't hear the service. She could barely make herself look at Brian before they closed the casket for the final time. *He looks like a wax replica sleeping in a public place. He is no longer the Brian I loved. My Brian is gone.*

It was finally over, and the last of the mourners left Brian's childhood home. Marny thought *soon they would have to do all of this for me, but I don't care. Brian is gone and nothing else matters.*

"Spend the night here, Marny. You don't want to be alone tonight." Brian's mother thought Marny looked too thin in her little black dress. Marny hadn't been eating much, and she had been vomiting if she ate. Stress. Fatigue.

"No, I prefer to go home. The outpouring of kindness has overwhelmed me, but I need time by myself." Marny was firm because she wanted no argument from Brian's mother. Marny didn't need that. She needed solitude, surrounded by Brian's things. She needed time to plan her own end.

Buttoning her coat, Marny quietly slipped out the back door and into her car. She made the drive in twenty minutes and walked into the silent rooms she had shared with Brian. In the living room she curled into a fetal position in Brian's chair. She grabbed his quilt and wrapped herself like a cocoon so she could draw in the remnants of Brian's smell.

"Brian, I can't do this. We planned to be *for always*. I can't go on by myself." Sobs shook her for hours. Marny gave in to them. She had no fight left.

The cancer had been diagnosed only nine weeks ago. Brian complained of a tender spot on his abdomen so he went to the doctor. After a few simple tests that they thought would detect gall stones, Brian was diagnosed with stage four cancer. The doctors weren't sure of the origin of the cancer, but agreed he had so little time left, it seemed senseless to put him through more tests. The cancer was spreading like an out of control forest fire filling his lungs and most of his torso.

Numb, the couple told their families and friends. Every minute they had left together, they savored. Brian decided against chemo or radiation. Marny reluctantly agreed. She had secretly hoped for a miracle drug or experiment that would save him. Brian's mother was against non-treatment, but she acquiesced to her only son.

Secretly, Brian and Marny had Brian's sperm frozen so Marny could bear their child if she chose. Brian knew it would be good for Marny—something to look forward to. Marny wasn't sure she could go through an *in vitro* pregnancy alone. Brian prayed that when the time came, the procedure would be successful.

The moment Brian died, Marny knew she would not use the frozen sperm but take her own life instead.

Right after they told everyone about the cancer, Brian stopped working, and Marny took an extended leave of absence from her teaching position. They rented a beach house and made a pact not to mention cancer during their stay. The sad reality would come soon enough. The couple walked the beach holding hands. Brian proposed to Marny all over again. They cooked their favorite meals and considered baby names. They slept late and watched movies in bed in each other's arms. The time at the beach was over too soon as Brian became sicker.

At home Brian weakened every day, but he tried to organize his affairs and explain everything to Marny. She would hold her hands over her ears, and sing nonsense rather than listen to him talk about his imminent death. He would pull her arms down and make her listen.

"Brian, it won't matter. If you die, I plan to die, too."

Brian was shocked to hear Marny utter these words. "Marny, don't say that. What about our baby? You have the chance to live life to the fullest and be a great mom. You are the best thing that ever happened to me. You must live on for me, Marny. Promise me that you will."

"I don't know if I can make that promise, Brian. I don't want to go on without you"

"We got terrible news. The worst news ever. You're still in shock. Don't make any rash decisions now. You have to choose life, Marny. Give yourself some time to readjust your life."

Marny walked outside so Brian wouldn't see the tears welling up in her eyes. By the time he followed her out to the porch, she had gained control of herself. She felt nauseous at what life was handing them, but she smiled and challenged Brian to a hand of gin rummy.

That was the last night they played cards. Brian became too weak to sit up. He began coughing spells that left him gasping and in terrible pain. Marny somehow found the strength to look calm for Brian, but inside she was having panic attacks.

Often they just lay in bed together, slept, held each other, and talked softly. As Brian slept, Marny felt the bile rising in her throat. *How could this be happening?* Cancer happened to other people—not to someone strong and healthy who was only thirty years old. Marny slid out of Brian's arms and hurried to the bathroom—nauseous. Her retching brought forth nothing since she was barely eating. She nibbled with Brian when he felt like eating.

Brian's mom and Marny put Brian on Hospice so he could die at home. Marny took a firm stand because Brian's mom wanted him in the hospital.

Marny felt certain she and the Hospice nurses could give Brian the best care at home.

His end came much too soon. The pain was horrendous for Brian until he was placed on morphine. His labored breathing frightened Marny, but she hid her fear from Brian. He was most comfortable if Marny sat behind him leaning against the headboard. She supported him as she held him in a bear hug lifting his arms to ease his breathing. Marny whispered how much she loved him, how happy he made her, and how she wished a miracle would happen so he would get better. It was in this position, in their marriage bed, during the whispers that Marny felt Brian slump and stop breathing. There would be no resuscitation. The Hospice nurse called Brian's mother who made the rest of the necessary phone calls. Marny held Brian for almost an hour until it was time for the funeral home to take him away from her forever.

Again after everyone left but family and close friends, Marny threw up. Everyone told her it was okay and that she had been so brave for Brian.

Marny stayed at home imagining how she would end her life as she counted the painkillers. She had enough to do the job. The date she chose was on their fifth wedding anniversary, a month away. If she were found as if she were sleeping, she thought it would be easier on her family. Peace washed over Marny as she thought of dying in the same bed as Brian.

Marny went back to her teaching job to keep busy. She couldn't eat and kept vomiting. She wondered if something was drastically wrong. Her mother-in-law suggested she see a doctor, and Marny went to keep the peace.

The doctor wanted to X-ray her stomach. "Could you be pregnant?"

Shocked at the question she replied bluntly, "No, my husband's dead."

"Just to be sure, you'll need to take a pregnancy test."

Marny was irritated but urinated on the stick the nurse gave her. She left it sitting in the restroom and walked back to the doctor's examination room.

In a few minutes the doctor was back. "How long ago did your husband pass away?"

Marny answered, "Two weeks ago."

"Well, he left you a present. You're pregnant."

"That can't be . . . He was so sick . . . We didn't . . . Are you positively sure? Can I take another?" Marny couldn't manage to spit out anything that sounded intelligent.

"The test you took is very accurate, but we'll do a blood test to make sure. You must be surprised, but now we have an explanation for your vomiting which will be gone in about a month." The doctor seemed pleased with himself—like he had created this baby.

Marny felt irritated. *I'm going to kill myself in less than a month. Can I kill our child, too?* "Do you need to do anything else or can I go?"

"I want you to take prenatal vitamins. I'll write a prescription. The nausea usually ends with the first trimester. Saltine crackers help in the morning. You are too thin which is understandable after what you have been through, but you have to eat more. I know it sounds like a cliché, but you are eating for two. Eat breakfast, lunch, and dinner, and a couple of snacks a day. You want a healthy birth weight baby."

Marny must have looked shell-shocked. "We have some pamphlets you can read that would explain a healthy prenatal diet."

She walked to the nurses' station and picked up the prescription and the pamphlet. "Do you want to take another pregnancy test?" the nurse asked.

"No, I'll buy one when I pick up the vitamins."

Marny walked to her car mumbling. "I guess I conceived this baby while we were at the beach. We didn't use birth control. I thought he was so sick that . . . Well, I thought wrong. This is incredible."

She didn't remember driving to the pharmacy. She was shocked when she pulled into the parking lot. She sat in her car deciding whether to go in.

Marny now had a bigger problem than she ever imagined. She could take her own life, but could she take the life of an innocent baby? Brian's baby? Marny professed to being pro-choice, but if she was faced with the situation of an unplanned pregnancy, she knew she could not go through with an abortion. *Was suicide the same as abortion?*

"What are the chances? My husband dies, I decide to commit suicide, and now I'm pregnant with his child. It must have happened that first week at the beach house." *After that Brian was just too tired. Snuggling, but no sex.*

Marny got out of her car and walked to the back of the store where the pharmacy was located. She placed her vitamin prescription on the counter. The female pharmacist smiled knowingly at Marny and rubbed her own pooching belly as she picked up the prescription. Marny paid and left with the vitamins. She did not buy a pregnancy test.

At home Marny sat in Brian's chair and thought about her current situation. *We did have his sperm frozen so I could choose to have our child if I wanted. Why did I go along with him if I didn't want it? I know Brian wanted it. I know his mom will be thrilled beyond words. But can I do this? Can I be a decent single mother to this little child trying to grow in my half-starved body?*

The answer was obvious, but she wasn't ready to admit it yet. *If I do decide to go through with the pregnancy, I'd better start eating right. A few vitamins won't cut it. This baby needs nourishment. Our baby needs a chance to be healthy.*

Once she had uttered the word 'our', she knew her decision had been made. She felt Brian's presence beside her in his chair, and tears spilled down her face. "Hey, Brian, sweetie, we're going to have a baby!"

Marny walked into the bathroom and flushed several bottles of Brian's painkillers.

After the baby shower, as Marny placed the new clothes neatly in Brian's old baby dresser, life began to make sense. *It would never be okay that Brian's life was snuffed out much too soon. Marny would always miss him, but with time and the arrival of the baby, life could be good again — in a different way. She realized that conceiving this baby was a true miracle that saved her life.*

She might even consider using a sperm bank deposit once she learned how to be a good mommy.

Life throws many curves that are unfair, but then, almost magically, life sends a straight-across-the-plate homerun pitch. You just have to swing, hit it, and run those bases around to home plate.

Home is the key word. Marny and Brian had a home together, and Marny would never let their child forget his daddy was part of their home.

Did Marny ever regret her decision? Never! Oh, by the way, the ultrasound showed that the baby was a boy—Brian Junior.

Lynne Gregg is the co-author of the middle-grade novel *Shake on it and Spit in the Dirt* and numerous magazine articles. She is a 15 year survivor of cancer and working on a novel concerning her experiences. She has been an invaluable member of the Houston Writers Guild for more than 16 years.

Casserole Confession

Nikki Loftin

Thirty years later, I can still recall the frozen horror that filled the kitchen that Sunday. I know it was my mother who reached out for the Parmesan cheese and instead grabbed hold of the Comet cleanser. But who placed it there? Me? My sister? What well-meaning idiot set the Pyrex casserole dishes, steaming from the oven, so close to the sink?

It didn't matter. My mother's hand shook, and the blue-white powder that flew out of the wide perforations on the metal lid sifted down in an unholy, unclean swath across the top of our Sunday dinner.

The mingled smells of chicken tetrazzini and powdered bleach filled the room. Then, a fraught pause. The only sounds were masculine voices in the living room, the men who were watching television and waiting impatiently for their Sunday dinner. Even as a child, I was annoyed when the men didn't help cook or clean. I wanted to be one of them, out there, lazing around, waiting to be waited on. Until that Sunday.

That afternoon, standing stock-still in the kitchen, three generations of women were transformed. A suburban mother, a doting grandmother, two impressionable daughters — changed forever. In that instant we became - the Borgias, Poisoners of men.

"Nobody says a word," Mama Lucrezia whispered, and she shot my sister and me a razor look. We nodded. "We can fix this."

Of course Mom could fix it; I never doubted it for an instant. She could whip up a ballet costume at a moment's notice, build doll house furniture by hand, play a half dozen instruments and make two weeks' worth of groceries last for a month. She was and is one of the most competent women I have ever known, capable of anything.

Capable of committing a culinary felony, too, as it turned out. Possibly, I thought, we were going to poison every one of the men in the next room.

I had never been so glad to be a girl.

"Go tell your father lunch won't be ready for twenty more minutes," Grandma instructed my sister. She ran out of the kitchen.

Grandma looked at my mom. Mom nodded. Not a word spoken, but perfect understanding. Mom picked up the nine by thirteens one at a time and carefully scraped a spoon across the top, removing most of the Comet. Not all of it, of course. That would have been impossible. Grandma blew at the last stubborn streaks, but the cream-of-mushroom soup was doing its job too well, holding everything together: chicken, spaghetti, olives, cheese, and abrasive cleanser. The casseroles were now, the can taunted, 1.2% sodium dichloro-s-triazinetrione dihydrate. Delicious *and* perfect for removing stubborn stains.

Mom raised an eyebrow. Grandma answered: "Cheese. Lots of cheese."

I grated cheddar until my arms ached. So did my sister, both of us struggling not to dissolve into maniacal laughter at the crime we were covering up. Who knew it would be such fun to plan a potential mass murder? A good friend will help you move, the saying goes, while a best friend will help you move a body. We were closer than best friends, my grandma, my mother, my sister and I. I remember with utter clarity Grandma giggling, "Oh! If Papa ever finds out!" If Papa *survives*, I thought.

The casseroles went back in the oven to melt the cheese. The broccoli, wilted beyond recognition, was placed on the table alongside white rolls that had gone dark brown on top from baking too long.

The meal, when it was served, was a strange affair. The men – my father, grandfather, and younger brother – tore into the food with gusto. I watched them lift steaming, glistening, cheese-covered, possibly fatal forkfuls of dinner to their mouths. Could they taste it? Would they get sick? Fall over at the table, pointing forks of blame at us as they perished?

The criminals watched from behind plates piled high with overcooked broccoli and burnt rolls. Our Lilliputian servings of casserole were scraped into the sink after the meal. I imagined the blades of the garbage disposal shining bright silver from the extra polish.

No one died, of course. No one even got sick. And it may be a strange way to think of it, but I remember that as one of the very first times my mother taught me a lesson I've relied on through illness, death, divorce and dinner parties gone wrong: You can fix anything with family togetherness, laughter, and a pound of cheddar.

Nikki Loftin is the author of *The Sinister Sweetness of Splendid Academy* (Razorbill) soon to be followed by its sequel. She writes essays, poetry, novels, and short stories. Her work has appeared in *Boy's Life, Pockets, Front Range Review*, and *Chicken Soup for the Soul*. She lives in Austin with her husband, surrounded by dogs, chickens, rattlesnakes and small, loud boys.

The Rebirth of Rose

Annie Daylon

There comes a single instant, a freeze-frame moment between old and new, known and unknown, when the drumbeat of indecision abruptly ceases and the stillness hangs like an unresolved chord, waiting for its cue to slide to resolution.

Rose stood in the center of living room, staring at the opaque, indestructible glass of the fire escape window. She smirked. *Escape.* There was no escape; the window had been painted shut. She fingered her breakout tool, a pilfered butter knife and contemplated — scrape paint, raise window, slip through.

Time was limited. Yes, he was gone overnight, but, at dawn, a jangle of keys, the harbinger of his return, would reach her eardrums. She glanced toward the door and trembled. To this point, she had gotten away with a few tiny deviations from his set of rules, from his idea of perfectionism. But this? This would not go unnoticed. What if she failed? She winced, remembering her last transgression, a minor infraction; her ribs still ached.

Rose's eyes flooded. She choked back a sob and wiped her tears on her sleeve. How had she ended up here? In this situation? She inched toward the window and hovered near the ledge, rocking from one foot to the other. How *had* she ended up here? Despite the awareness that her porthole of time was eroding, Rose caved to her overpowering need to comprehend. She continued to stand and sway as her mind replayed her journey from her beginning to her now. Memories gushed forth like the waters of Niagara.

The early years: Mother's lullaby . . . *Hush Little Baby, don't say a word* . . . The squishy, brown teddy bear with the pink bow tie. The alphabet blocks stacked into a pyramid. The first, soggy Valentine left at the door in the rain. The shiny new black patent leather shoes that pinched her toes. The friends: red-headed Janie and brown-skinned Chris and blue-eyed Mary. The games: *You're it* and *Simon Says* and *Hop Scotch*. Kicking high on swings, wind tossing her hair. Reading Dr. Seuss, rhymes tripping her tongue. Making mud pies, dirt blackening her fingernails.

School days: The whisper of lead pencils sliding across paper. The specks of chalk dust dancing in sunlight. The ping of the desk bell relaying *Time's up*. So many multiplication tables, repeated like bird song. The very first poem: *There was a little turtle, he lived in a box . . .* The piano recital: *Beethoven's Fur Elise.* Weekly choir practice: *Doh, re, mi, fa, sol . . .*

On and on, through primary, elementary, junior, and senior. Ah, high school . . . giggling and dating. Meeting boys. Loving boys. Dropping boys. Dropping prom dress for promise of everlasting love. Promise broken, heart broken, moving on to cap-and-gown.

Adulthood: Still more school. Two universities. Two degrees. A career in teaching. Struggling in the first classroom, learning her craft, paying her dues. Achieving self-assurance. Guiding her students—laughing, wide-eyed children— in the ways of freedom and confidence and independence.

Rose, the classroom teacher, a roll she relished both in school and out. Shoulders low, back straight, head elevated. *Look at me.* Soft-spoken and deliberate. Aware that, at parties and meetings, all present were waiting for her to utter each carefully chosen word, each elongated phrase, knowing they were longing for some sign of punctuation that would indicate the end of her turn, the start of theirs. But, cognizant, perhaps cruel, she would inhale sharply—a well-practiced device that made people pause before jumping in; then she would smile, and continue on her chosen topic.

Rose was in control, completely in control, her life spiraling upward, onward. All the while, she maintained independence. Conquering all. Needing no one. Accessorizing with and then casting aside lovers and friends alike. Family? Out of touch. Rose, alone. Just Rose. Under the assumption that she would always be this way. Free. Independent.

Then Rose met Vincent.

One July morning at the farmers' market, having just barely crawled out of her daily mug of coffee, Rose met Vincent. Actually, she bumped him with the shopping basket that was suspended from the crook of her arm. When she turned toward him to utter a brief apology, she dropped the melon she was holding and blinked into his face.

No man could be, should be, so perfect. His eyes, iridescent as opals, impaled her. Her body flashed with desire, molten lava, churning, whirling, surging. He stepped toward her, close, too close by her standard of personal space, yet she didn't shrink away. She moved in until she could feel the heat of his breath slide down her neck. Instinctively, her fingers flew to her throat. He took her hand and kissed it. He owned her in that second. She knew it. She bowed to it. Would she, could she, ever be good enough for this eidolon of masculinity?

He stepped back and apologized for perhaps being too forward. He could not help but succumb to the temptation that was her beauty, he had said in honeyed tones. She melted into the compliment. And later, that same day, she melted into his body. In his home. In his bed. A single night that turned into days. Within weeks, she was living there, planning never to leave.

And, in fact, she never did leave. There was no need, he said. No need for her to work for he had money. No need for her to go anywhere for he would bring all to her. No need for her to do anything but simply *be*. There. With him. In his luxurious loft. High above the city.

Vincent's loft was indeed luxurious. And spacious and shiny. Amazingly shiny. Glistening with stainless steel counters and cupboards and appliances. Shinier still was the metal ductwork that defined the perimeter of the sixteen-foot ceiling. Lighting was provided by center lines of fluorescents which glared at night, flooding the three-thousand-square-foot space. All the windows were opaque (for extra privacy, Vincent explained) but daylight was escorted into the loft by nine sun tunnels, set into the roof in *Tic Tac Toe* formation. So high up, those skylights, thought Rose. Inaccessibly high.

Rose was initially in awe of the loft, and everything in it, especially the spotless kitchen with its completely-stocked pantry. All grocery items were in ABC order, literally. Every label faced front and the lid of each can gleamed. Beside the door to the pantry, there was a steel rack for dish towels—two, ironed, linen dish towels—which hung perfectly straight, bottoms aligned. Even the cutlery drawer, utensils nested in glistening groups of eight, was spotless—nary a crumb.

When Vincent was home, Vincent was cleaning. He insisted on teaching her his maintenance methods, and would keep teaching her, he said, until he was certain she could clean properly. Together, they murdered many an evening doing nothing but dusting. Though she smiled as he guided her through the regimen of cleaning, she was aware of something pinging at her brain. Wasn't this all a bit twisted . . . this excessive compulsion for cleanliness, for perfection? Maybe. Yet, she went along with it. He was so perfect. She, too, would strive to be perfect. Like him. For him. When she became perfect, she would be worthy of his love.

Once, only once, did she voice the idea of leaving the loft, of going out . . . just for a morning of shopping. He laughed a dismissive laugh and waved the idea away. The next morning, she awoke to find herself in handcuffs. Shiny, polished handcuffs. Just a joke, he had said, removing the cuffs and sliding the key into his back pocket. Someday, when she was ready, she could go out, he told her. Not yet.

If only she had run then, but no, she had dismissed the sick feeling that had taken up residence in her gut. She merely rubbed her wrists and smiled. He loved her so much; he couldn't bear for her to be away from his home . . . that's all it was. Her reasoning was reaffirmed later in the day when he brought her a brilliant bouquet of roses, blood-red roses. She silenced her urge to scream and concentrated on his kindness. The rose, her namesake flower, was a symbol of pure love and deep passion. It was thoughtful of him to give her roses.

A few days later, he hit her . . . but it was open-handed, a slap, not a punch. He was under stress, a high-powered business man, and she had broken a cardinal rule. She knew she should not borrow his things, yet she had. Yes, she had used his shaving cream. Yes, she had wiped the can clean and she had returned it to its place. But she hadn't turned the label to the front. He, being perfect, noticed this oversight. He liked things to be perfect. She deserved the slap; it was condign punishment. She resolved to be better, for him.

Every day, she scrubbed, buffed, and straightened. Trying to achieve perfection. Every day, he inspected. Usually, she passed. Occasionally, she erred. Always, when judgment was pending, anxiety hung over her like a cloud of black flies awaiting the signal to inject her body with venomous welts. The judgment and the corrections were, she reasoned, a necessary part of her training. When she was perfect she would be deserving of him. She was willing to continue, status quo, until that time arrived.

But, one day, an anomaly occurred.

As he was examining the kitchen, as she was waiting, she glanced at the towel rack and realized that the towels were not aligned; one was hanging at least three centimeters below the other. Her legs weakened. *Oh god.* How had she missed it? The last time she had made an error, she had spent hours locked up, curled like a comma in the large, shiny, stainless steel dog kennel that he had brought home, just for her. *Oh, god.* Maybe she could slip over and fix the towel. She dug her nails into her palm. *Oh, god.* He turned. She braced herself for a blow.

But, smiling through perfect teeth, he merely slid by her, stroked her hair and padded down the hall toward his office. Her eyes popped wide. He hadn't noticed. She raced to adjust the towels, took a deep breath and exhaled in a whoosh. Problem solved.

Relief stayed with her for hours but the incident niggled at her for days. How had *he* missed it? *She* made mistakes, yes. But he did not. How had *he* missed it? She obsessed, repeating the question like a mantra. How? How? How? If he missed it, then maybe he wasn't perfect. Maybe there were other things he wouldn't notice. But what other things? Maybe something small—a tissue, a crumpled tissue—strategically placed, on the floor, beside the toilet. Maybe she should try that, just to check. Did she dare?

It took her a few days to get up the nerve to carry out a small test. When she finally did, and the tissue went unnoticed, she got braver. She hid a butter knife. Would he realize that there were only seven in the cutlery drawer?

She waited. He opened the drawer; he closed the drawer. He went to his office. She pumped her fist into the air and resisted the urge to dance. Immediately, she returned the knife but vowed to try again. Next time, she would raise the stakes.

Two days later, she took another knife and poked at the paint on the window ledge. She scraped away three tiny shavings and left them on the floor by the window. He didn't notice them. Aha! Proof. She had solid proof now. Mr. Perfect wasn't so perfect. Maybe there was no such thing as perfectionism after all. Maybe perfectionism was an illusion.

All this time, she had been trying to please him, to be perfect for him. Never questioning him. Never discussing it with others. But, wait a minute! There were no others. How had she not realized that Vincent had deliberately kept her in complete isolation? There was no phone, other than the cell he carried in his pocket. No one came to the loft. Ever. Had he no friends? No family? She had just always assumed that he was independent. Just as she was independent.

Independent? What about the red marks on her wrists, evidence of the now frequent wearing of handcuffs? Independent? Yes, she *was* independent, completely free, of family and friends. But she was *totally* dependent on Vincent.

Anger ignited in her gut and hemorrhaged through her pores as she recalled yesterday when she was confined in the kennel. With a voice as plaintive as an oboe, she had begged him for food. Finally, after she curled into a fetal position and cried for hours, he relented, released her, and led her to the pantry. Then, generously, he permitted her to choose whatever gift of food she desired.

How the hell had she let this happen?

There comes a single instant when the drumbeat of indecision ceases . . .

Rose looked down at the window ledge. With a start, she realized that while she had been reliving, remembering, regurgitating, she had also been prying, poking, scraping at the hardened paint. A jumble of paint shavings lay huddled on the ledge; many more formed a scatter graph on the hardwood floor. There would be no hiding this. He would know that she had tried to escape. This was it. This was the moment, the event horizon. There was no turning back.

She released the knife and it clattered to the floor. She tugged and jiggled the window. It resisted. Her heart raced like a formula one car as she increased her efforts. She shook and pulled and throttled and sobbed. No joy. She wiped the sweat from her brow and went at it again. At last, the window flew open. She shrank back, startled, as pigeons fluttered from the outside ledge and took to the sky. Night air gushed into the room and on its heels, the blare of traffic, the flash of neon, the stench of exhaust. She leaned over the sill to take in the sounds and smells.

A sudden jangling of keys sounded behind her, piercing the cacophony of the city and causing her heart to leap into overdrive. She gasped and, ignoring a stab of pain in her injured ribs, jumped through the window, onto the fire escape. Her hands grasped the railing and she paused. A millisecond hesitation. Just long enough for her to notice that dawn had splintered the horizon.

Drawn to the light, compelled by the light, she propelled her way down the narrow steps of the fire escape like a newborn navigating a birth canal. When her feet touched sidewalk — the dirty, imperfect sidewalk — she raced nonstop to the east, to the light, to a new life. She did not look back.

Annie Daylon lives in Canada and is the author of *Maggie of the Marshes* and *Passages, a Collection of Short Stories.*

The Bird in the Bush

Carolyn Thorman

Dinner was included in Taken-Alive's rent, but when Hedy served the old Indian kielbasa or cabbage rolls, he slid away his plate. So tonight, when she fixed corn pudding, he lowered his spoon and said, "For a Polack, your Kickapoo food's not half bad."

Taken-Alive had moved into the top floor of the Petroky's after his apartment building in South Houston was condemned. He had come to the city from the reservation at Eagle Pass to work in the refineries. Pensioned, he spent his days on the front steps watching the comings and goings of Billings Street. Nothing got by him: Hedy sensed he was even aware of her husband's screw ups, and of the grief they caused.

Lately, every day after work, her husband Cash would stride past Taken-Alive on the steps of his own house and bound up the steps of Bora Slovonajak's place next door. Pushy, that woman. First off, the day she moved in, she spotted Cash in the yard and asked to borrow a hammer. He insisted on nailing up her curtain rods himself. The next thing Hedy knew, he was replacing Bora's porch railings. Don't forget, I'm carpenter," he said.

"So charge her," Hedy said.

Cash had spent weeks building Bora a bookcase, answering Hedy's complaints with a sullen silence. When first married, twenty years ago, Cash and Hedy could talk, kid around. But the years seemed to have smothered his humor with a gray, furry mold.

Taken-Alive tore a piece of fry-bread in half. "How's the wood-working next door coming along?"

"Almost finished. But now it's her fuse-box, too."

The sound of boots on the porch, the opening of a door, and the herbal smell of wood shavings filled the room. Hedy looked up at Cash's tanned jaw, the lean muscles under his Polo shirt, and as usual, her breath quickened.

Cash called over his shoulder, "I told you, come right on in."

Bora stood in the doorway, one hand on her hip. "Am barging, but Cash said all right."

Hedy eyed her neighbor's fluffy brown hair, teeth white against plum lipstick, and saw herself through Bora's eyes: a dowdy, skinny housewife in her husband's old shirt.

"This little lady's got no electric," Cash said. "Fuse box disaster. Think we can rustle up some dinner?" He motioned to the table. "There's Mister Taken-Alive. You seen him on the steps." He opened the refrigerator and yelled, "Who's for firewater?"

Taken-Alive winced. Hedy reached around Cash and pulled out three Lone-Stars and set one in front of the old man. Cash hovered over Bora and began pouring her beer into a tall glass.

Hedy turned to Bora and forced a smile. "You Hungarian?"

"Albanian." She slid a gold horse back and forth along a chain around her neck.

"Then you must know the Rabovics," Hedy said.

Bora laughed. "Got here from Canada. No work up there."

A Gypsy, this one, Hedy thought. "What do you do?"

Bora finished her beer and wiped her mouth on her sleeve. "Waitress, sometimes dancer, sometimes whatever."

"Should be no problem finding work like that in Houston," Hedy said.

"Try with no green-card."

Cash held a spoon filled with corn pudding over Bora's plate. "She's got visa problems up the kazoo. Some brush with the Toronto cops."

Bora laughed. "Meth brush."

Cash reddened and glanced at Taken-Alive.

"You're not worried about mentioning dope?" Hedy asked.

Bora shrugged. "What's done is done."

Her eyes moving from Bora, to Cash, then back to Bora, Hedy sat back and eased off her sandals. Cash had always had problems — had been a problem. When Joe, their only kid, went into the army, Cash took off for Seattle. "To get my head straight," he put it. Months later he came back homesick and broke. Hedy baby-sat the neighbors' kids until he got on his feet. Then it was antiques, then the water-purification franchise ... Taken-Alive's rent was re-booting the savings account.

Growing up in Warsaw, Hedy had learned that no matter what you built, someone came along to tear it down. Life was a matter of renovation, no more, no less.

After her fourth beer, Bora leaned across the table to light Take-Alive's cigarette and dropped the burning match into the ashtray. "Whoops," she said.

"Careful," Hedy said as the flame smoldered and died.

"Time for this little girl to go home." Bora lifted her sequined handbag and struggled to her feet. Cash, his hand on her elbow, started across the kitchen and Hedy grabbed the back of his shirt.

"Helping her," he said.

"To next door?"

Cash faced her. "Don't tailgate me."

"You come right back."

"As a matter of fact," he said quietly, "I just might never come back at all."

Later, Hedy stared into the back yard listening to the kids in the alley shout, "One, two three, one, two three." The moon hung above the EuroSpan Building, a block away. She wasn't born yesterday. These things happen. But only to people like the no-account Stotly's, to movie stars, to French people. Taken-Alive came up beside her. His hair, held with a silver barrette at the nape of his neck, fell in a thick, black mane.

"Why would God let this woman destroy my home?" she asked.

"So you can rebuild it. Get some sleep."

She roamed the kitchen, then lay down on the daybed in the sun porch. Restless, she got up and went to the front door. For some reason she opened it. Smells of creosote blew in from the Gulf. The streetlight cast shadows of leaves on the pavement. She looked at the footprints of Cash's boots on her clean cement steps, at his oily heel marks. Grease, sure enough. She got a bucket from the broom closet, filled it with water and a shot of ammonia to kick up the Mr. Clean. The fumes made her gag, but the soap did the trick. A squad car pulled up along the curb. The cop lowered the window and called, "Why are you scrubbing the sidewalk?"

"Getting rid of the dirt before it sets."

He watched for a minute, shook his head and gunned the motor.

She wrung out the rag, an old tee-shirt soft as wet bread. She looked up at Bora's window, at the peeling frame and drawn blinds, the glass rain-streaked, as if tears had run down from the roof.

The smell of damp wool, and a soft weight fell across her shoulders. Taken Alive straightened the blanket and led her inside. Her fingers were puckered from the water and her skin had swollen over her wedding ring. Although it made her sweat, she held onto the blanket as she lay down on the sofa.

The clock on the mantel struck one. Moonlight poured through the curtains. Her hands smelled of Mr. Clean. Eyes burning, she wondered if she would ever sleep again. A squeak of the floorboards and Taken-Alive said, "Here."

Propped on one elbow, she took the glass of water he offered and studied the white capsule he held in his palm. "What is it?"

"For the pain."

When she awoke, sun dappled the beige carpet. Smells of coffee came from the hall. The refrigerator door slammed and Cash whistled in the kitchen. The misery of last night picked up where it left off. Cash was buttering a bagel, his eyes red, his chin bristling with ashy stubble. A knight appliquéd on the breast pocket of his shirt hung by a thread. Hedy went to the stove and tipped the coffee pot.

Cash jumped up. "I'll fix more."

She waited until he turned off the tap. "Why weren't you home?"

He held the pot midair. "I got to take it from the beginning." He opened the cupboard, lifted out a can of coffee, crossed the kitchen, and started rummaging in a drawer.

"Can opener's in the top right," she said.

"Bora's cousin giving her a job in Ohio," he said. "She needs me to go with her."

Something inside Hedy disconnected causing her stomach to float. "When?"

"Don't give me no third degree."

Anger hit her like the heat when she opened the oven. "You got responsibilities."

"Joe's in the army."

"So I'm in the garbage?"

He snapped on the burner. "I'll send money regular."

"Where will you get it?" She looked up at the statue of Our Lady of Sorrows on the windowsill. Every week Cash slipped his paycheck under its ceramic base. "What happened," she asked. "To make you run with that tramp?"

"I want a new life."

Her throat burned. "What's wrong with the one you got?" He picked at the knight on his shirt. "I feel sick," she said.

He slammed his fist on the stove. "Don't make it no harder for me."

"Animal," she shouted.

She forced herself to calm down. Slowly, deliberately she picked up the ashtray Bora had used the night before and dumped the contents in the garbage, a butt smeared with plum lipstick leering up at her. "I'm taking out the trash," she said. As she pushed past him, he dropped the knight on the counter.

A mourning dove cooed from a telephone wire. She walked along the hollyhocks flanking the drive. Turning onto the street brought her to the front of her house. The old Indian sat at his post. "The mister's leaving," she said.

Taken-Alive tapped his cigarette ash into the potted geranium. "He'll be back."

"Fifty years old and that gypsy made up his mind."

"That's when a man finds out he's tall as he'll ever grow."

"She gave him high-ideas."

"You don't look so hot. Had breakfast?"

"Ever see anyone like that Albanian?"

"Not in Eagle Pass." He flipped his cigarette into the street and stood. "Let's go."

She strolled along beside him. "No green card." The thought that caught in her mind was swelling into a full-blown idea. "Say I turn her in. Immigration," she went on, "sent Veronica Spassky back to the Ukraine after her ex ratted. She never stood a chance. Especially after they got the tip, searched her place and found hash."

Taken-Alive held the door of the Pizza Paradise and motioned her to a booth. Hedy, picturing Bora in handcuffs, smiled and sat down.

The waiter brought the pizza and iced tea they ordered and headed into the back room. Taken-Alive stared at the molten tomato sauce as if it held wisdom, the right words. "If you were my daughter, I'd order you to lay off the immigration business."

Hedy blew on a forkful of mozzarella. "My only chance," she said.

"For what? Keep your tent wrapped around his pole?"

"He's my life."

"Do your own. You said you were a nurse in Poland?"

"Years ago. I came to the States when I was twenty-two." She sighed. "But who hires an unlicensed nurse who hasn't practiced in years?"

Taken-Alive thought for a minute, laughed, and said, "The Indian Health Service."

When she got back to the house, a note from Cash was propped against the napkin holder. Unrelated thoughts rolled through her mind. Not Ohio this soon; his aunt's wedding coming up, the bowling tournament. She took the sheet of tablet paper and read aloud. "The electric's still off. Taking the camper to Galveston. Be back Sunday. Don't worry about the Coleman lamp." She folded the note slowly and looked around the kitchen. The knight lay on the counter, its eye staring at the crack in the ceiling.

That afternoon she painted the porch chairs yellow. Taken-Alive ate dinner alone while she unclogged leaves from the gutter with a rake handle. At midnight, the thought of the desolate bedroom drove her to make up the daybed in the sun porch. As the clock struck two she was still imagining Cash and Bora on the bunk in the camper. Her insides were shredded flesh, as if the machinery that pumped, soothed and digested had been ripped out. At three, her skin still clammy, she recalled Taken-Alive's pills and threw off the covers.

Snores floated through his door. "Mr. Alive," she called. "Got a minute?"

Shuffling, then the door opened. He was in a gray jogging suit with red stripes down the sides.

"Can't sleep," she said. I wonder if that pill . . ."

She waited and he returned with an open three-pound coffee can and tipped it toward her.

"What are they?"

"Snowflakes."

"Where'd you get them?"

He held a finger to his lips.

"Thank you very much," she said, as if accepting a dinner mint.

The idea assembled before she got back to the sun porch. She turned on one foot, ran back and banged on his door. He opened it. "Sell me those," she said.

He grabbed her shoulders. "Put that out of your mind."

"No, not for me. To plant on the gypsy tomorrow before I go to immigration."

He shook his head. "You're getting in too deep."

Hedy thought out the details as she explained them. "Bora's place is like ours. Know that back door that goes into the garage? Has a window I can bust and reach around to the handle."

"Fooling with immigration's one thing, breaking and entering's another. You'll wind up in jail."

"How much for the flakes?"

"Friends don't sell to friends." He closed his eyes and nodded, as if having come to a conclusion. "I'll give you some. But in the morning. And I'm going with you to see where those pills wind up."

"You don't trust me."

"Or your crazy ideas. Besides, nice ladies don't know how to break windows."

Her throat tightened. "Thanks," she said.

The next night Hedy was tying on a plastic rain cap when Taken-Alive came into the kitchen. He wore a black nylon shirt: the headband that circled his forehead was fastened at the nape of his neck, a few eagle feathers hanging from the knot. "Never too late to change your mind," he said.

"Won't take but a minute."

He sighed and handed her a small zip-lock bag filled with capsules. "We'll need a flashlight."

"The mister took the Coleman, but get what you need from the shed out back."

Taken-Alive burst back inside the kitchen, wiping his feet on the doormat. "It's coming down buckets."

"I'll get umbrellas."

"Slow us down. Let's get this over with."

Rain from her hat ran in to her eyes. In the dark she almost knocked over a birdbath the last tenant left in Bora's yard. She was finally able to make out the narrow wooden door and its top panel of glass. "Stand back," Taken-Alive said.

A crash and the sound of falling shards blended with the rain. Taken-Alive lowered the hammer. The smell of a moldy garage filled the air as she followed him around pyramids of paint cans, garden tools and a stepladder missing its lower rungs. Cautiously, Taken-Alive opened the kitchen door. The room was partially lit by the streetlight, and a stray moonbeam. "Where do the pills go?" he asked.

"I think in with her clothes."

He had just played the flashlight over the stairs, and swung it onto the floor when a voice screamed, "Vodka."

She froze.

The next "Vodka" was followed by a squawk.

"A bird," Taken-Alive said on his way to a bedroom. He paused, bent over and lifted up a yard-long chain. She raised her head to follow the cone of light as it flit over a high rattan cage with pillows on its floor, onto the smaller cage bouncing from an arched hanger bolted to the wall, along a mattress on the floor, up and over a velour tiger-striped throw.

"Vodka."

A black swastika was painted on a sheet tacked on the wall. Taken-Alive snapped off the flashlight. She reached for it, and he said, "I've seen enough."

She drew back the velvet drapes covering the window. An incense-burner rested on the sill. The room was lit by the greenish light of the streetlamp. Taken-Alive nodded at the swastika. "Your people have strange beliefs."

She thought of Warsaw, the posters with German slogans still on the underpass of the Poniatowski Bridge. One depicted the Polish falcon in flames. Another, an Aryan princess gazing at a soldier.

"Let's get out of here," Taken-Alive said.

She took the zip-lock bag from her pocket. It seemed heavier than it had been minutes before. "I think I don't want any part of this," she said more to herself than to Taken-Alive. She slipped the bag back in her raincoat and headed toward the hall. Voices from outside seemed to be coming closer. The downstairs door slammed and Cash's words rose from the stairway. "Power, or no power, I'm damned glad we got rained out."

Bora whimpered something.

"And I ain't going to no Ohio, neither."

"You promised."

Hedy looked around. "Hide," she whispered to Taken-Alive.

Now Cash was on the landing, yelling at Bora, "Give me the lamp." He lifted the Coleman, "What the—"

"We're leaving," Hedy said.

Cash flung out his arm. "Hold your horses."

Bora slipped around them, took a candle from the nightstand and a packet of matches from her jeans. The candle lit a photo of her, naked, arm around a statue of a Canadian Mountie. "I was a blonde, then," she said, then giggled.

Cash turned to Hedy, "Get on up to the house."

"Vodka."

"That's my bird," Bora said. She staggered and bent her head to light her cigarette from the candle. "Named Vodka."

Hedy was halfway into the hall when she heard a crackling sound. She turned just in time to see the spark land on the throw, then the mattress shoot up in flames.

Cash yelled, "Look what you've gone and done."

Taken Alive tore the sheet from the wall and began beating at the fire.

Creamy smoke rose from the bedding. "I'm outta here," Cash shouted.

"Vodka."

She managed to reach up and unhook the cage, Vodka an anthracite lump on the bottom. "Mr. Alive," Hedy shouted, and ran to Bora on the floor.

"Lift her feet," Taken-Alive said. They got Bora out of the way of the flaming carpet with no time to spare.

"Is she dead?" Hedy asked.

"Drunk."

Outside, sirens screamed. A voice from a bullhorn boomed, "Jump."

Hedy, hanging on to the birdcage, wiped her streaming eyes on her sleeve. She stumbled to the window and stuck out her head.

"We got a net down here," a fireman called.

Hedy called back, "It's only the bedroom. We'll be out the front door." She caught up with Taken-Alive dragging Bora across the landing. The birdcage bumped against her legs as she made her way down, while a fireman, arms around a throbbing hose, took the steps two at a time.

"Coming through," he yelled, slamming her against the wall.

"Watch out."

"Sorry, lady."

"Hey, Charlie, here's your victim."

Outside, Hedy paused to catch her breath. She handed the cage to a fireman who seemed baffled by the quivering bird inside. Cash sat on the curb. Three fire trucks, an ambulance and a squad car blocked the middle of the street. The rain had slacked off and the cement was rosy from the flares set up to re-route traffic. The double doors of the ambulance were opened wide enough for the gurney holding Bora, who was trying to sit up, straining against the straps.

Cash came over and stood beside Hedy and Taken-Alive. An attendant with a coffee stain on his white sleeve unsnapped the point of a pen. "You a relative?" he asked Cash.

"Neighbor. She don't have people around here."

"One of you got to come along and sign her into the hospital, taking her to Ben Taub," the attendant said. "Hop in."

Cash nodded to Hedy.

"I'm not sure—"she began.

"You always handle things," Cash said.

She moved forward, hesitated: her eyes blurred as she watched a vision float by behind them. She could actually see the minutes, days, and years to come, every bit as real, as visible as the rain that had just passed. And she realized that if she wanted to, she could spend the rest of her life walking one step ahead of Cash, knitting, and he would be two steps behind, unraveling. The words were not as hard to speak as she would have thought. How simple it was to say, "You're on your own."

The jump-seat beside the stretcher wobbled under his weight.

A few folks milled around the fire trucks while the men stowed the hoses. "I put the cage in the front lawn," a fireman said.

Hedy stared at her neighbor's house. The soggy mattress lay in the grass. Black sticks of rattan covered the steps. A kid kicked an empty bottle into the street, while a dog lapped water from the incense bowl. Bora's bedroom windows were black holes, the eyes of a skeleton.

Taken-Alive followed her into the kitchen. The room was silent. "Do you feel it?" he asked. "Riding the air – peace that flies through the window and builds a nest, thread by thread."

She drew a curtain panel aside and looked at the yard. "There's a bird out there." she said. Slim black stripes, the shadow of the cage, lay across the grass. She dropped the curtain, and turned to Taken-Alive. "Waiting to come in."

Nice Legs

Pamela Fagan Hutchins

My triathlon-loving husband is a native of St. Croix, U.S. Virgin Islands. Yah, mon. When he moved to Texas for me, he had to learn some Texas tricks, and this old dog didn't want to. It took a lot for him to find his inner Bubba-mon.

When we had lived in Texas less than two years, Eric and I celebrated our anniversary in Fredericksburg, a charming hamlet chock-a-full of German history in the Hill Country of Texas. Like anyone would, we planned our entire getaway around bicycling and running. However, given the fact that we'd just run the Texas marathon days before, it was very moderate bicycling and running.

Eric hadn't quite adjusted to Texas yet. Don't get me wrong. He liked Texas, but public outings with him scared me to death. Eric was always just a breath away from getting his ass whupped by a cowboy, because he is an incurable smartass.

Case in point: Eric and I met at work, and soon afterwards, he said to me, "Don't expect me to treat you like your shit doesn't stink just because everyone else here does." Charming. And then he asked me to marry him. I guess we know who won that round.

Where were we? Oh yes, driving through Llano on the way to Fredericksburg. We were in the heart of Texas deer hunting country, and it just happened that we were smack in the middle of deer hunting season. As we drove into town, Eric put on his thickest, most sarcastic drawl and estimated the IQ and body weight of each thermal-camouflage-clad, beer-bellied hunter we passed. We pulled up to a gas pump, surrounded by converted SUVs and ATVs tricked out with gun turrets and swiveling Lazy Boys in their hacked-off back ends.

Eric put the car in park. "You're going to have to pump the gas."

Not to be a princess, but, "'Scuse me?" My husband never lets me lift a dainty little finger if he can help it. He'd have to be vomiting up a lung to ask me to pump gas.

He gestured at his bare legs and running attire. "I can't go out there like this."

"Because it's too cold?" I could understand this, seeing as it was January and all. That's why I had on full-length running tights. Duh.

"No, because . . ." He jerked his head toward the nearest hunter, garbed head-to-toe to withstand an arctic blast. "People will stare at me."

"Ahhhhhhh."

Eric's shorts were truly short; you know, the kind that shows 99.9% of your thighs? You see shorts like these on real runners in city parks. You do not see them in Llano, Texas. In Llano, real men don't wear sissy running shorts. Hell, real men don't run at all, in short shorts or anything else. Real men don't need to run, unless it's to the Allsup's for a six-pack of Lone Star beer. They get their exercise the manly way — they hunt and field-dress deer after they poke their dogies and till the back forty on their John Deeres. (My apologies to all aforesaid real men, 'cause I know there's a difference between a farmer and a cowboy, and never the twain shall meet.)

Well, I may have giggled and made a comment or two at this point, I dunno, but I did pump the gas. We passed more hunters on our way to a café where we planned to meet my mother for breakfast, like anyone would on their anniversary trip . . . Um, yeah.

Anyway, Eric kept humming some dueling banjos song and talking about people who marry their first cousins. Then we pulled into the parking lot of the café.

Eric put the car in park. He turned a stricken face to me.

"Lotta hunters in there," I said before he had a chance to speak, gesturing towards the tiny, crowded restaurant and then at the giant vehicles around us. And I coughed to cover a chuckle.

"Har-de-har-har," said Eric.

"I think you're a little underdressed," I said, and this time I burst out laughing. Every person in the restaurant except my mom, who by now was waving cheerily at us through the window, was wearing thermal camo overalls.

We hurried into the bacon-scented café, Eric tugging in vain at his shorts. They were as long as they were going to get. All eyes followed us to the table, where Mom kissed and hugged us with noisy gusto.

As soon as we sat down, she asked Eric to run to her car and get something. Well, a man doesn't ever say no to his mother-in-law, does he? Eric took a deep breath and re-trod his walk of shame to the parking lot, wishing, I'm sure, for Harry Potter's invisibility cloak.

When he was out of earshot, I leaned in and whispered, "Mom, Eric is mortified about his running shorts."

"Why?" she asked. "He looks fine."

"Look around, Mom. Hunters. No short running shorts." I giggled. "He feels conspicuous."

My mother never wastes an opportunity, and the woman is quick. She turned to the nearest hunter, a healthy fellow of 270 pounds or so, 8.6 pounds of it in facial hair.

"Would you do me a favor?" she asked him.

Have I mentioned that my mother is a great source of genetic material? She is charming and pretty, and all men love her. This hunter was no exception.

"Why sure, ma'am, what can I do ya for?" he said, and damn if his voice wasn't a dead ringer for Eric's imitation hunter-drawl earlier.

"See that man in the running shorts out there in the parking lot? That's my son-in-law. He is a little embarrassed about wearing shorts. I was wondering if you could let out a big wolf whistle when he comes back in?"

He turned to his cronies, who were hanging on every word of this interchange. He brayed a laugh, and after a split second, so did his two friends. "I'd be delighted to help ya out, ma'am."

"Thank you sooooo much," she said, and turned back to her menu, a Mona Lisa smile on her face.

The front door opened, sounding its bell. My clean-shaven husband with his mighty fine exposed gams stepped in.

Without hesitating as long as it would take to load his 30.06 deer rifle, the hunter yelled out,

"Hey boy, NICE LEGS!"

Eric looked around slowly, hoping the hunter was talking to someone else. His face lost all color. The restaurant grew so quiet you could almost hear the steam hissing out of Eric's ears. After a few beats, the café exploded in sound, as the hunter and his buddies cackled and whooped with laughter. They pounded the table, and one of them clapped our hunter on the back with a resounding thwump.

Eric tilted his head just enough to be perceptible and made the four quick strides from the door to our table, his naked legs eye-level as he pushed between two tables on the way. The hunter reached out and clasped his meaty paw around Eric's arm.

He hooked his thumb at my mother. "Yore mother-in-law put me up to it. I don't normally comment on another feller's legs."

"They are awful nice, though," one of his friends said, and they all set to hee-hawing again.

It is possible that Eric now finds this story humorous. At the time, he may or may not have planned the slow and painful death of his mother-in-law in the near future, although you'd never have known it then. Let's just say that when we drew up our house plans for our someday house on our property in Nowheresville, he didn't include a mother-in-law suite.

But he did let me buy him a pair of longer running shorts.

Adapted from *Hot Flashes and Half Ironmans,* by Pamela Fagan Hutchins and reprinted with permission from SkipJack Publishing.

The Art of Ironing

Denise Ditto Satterfield

Wrapped up tightly in the plastic flower-covered shower curtain, I never felt so alone.

"Come on out from there and get in the bath," my new step-mother kept saying to me over and over. I didn't even know this woman, who I recently learned was my new mother, and she wanted me to take off my clothes and get into the bathtub with two little girls I didn't know either. Her children, but strangers to me. My own mother had never seen me naked – at least not that I could remember – and I had never, ever taken a bath with anyone else in my whole life.

As I slowly unrolled myself from my cocoon, these thoughts kept running through my head. Here I was, seven years old and my whole life had taken a turn for the worse.

I was living with these people now, some lady and her two kids. And not just two kids, but two daughters. Up until this time, I had been the only girl in my family and the baby. I had two older brothers, and I thought I had it made. I had my own room, my own bed, and my own radio. I loved my radio. All of that was over. Now, I had to sleep with these girls called step-sisters, in the same room, *the girls' room*, in the same bed and no radio.

I no longer had my identity. One sister was a year older than me and the other, a year younger. That made her the baby.

When my dad married Gloria, my world was shattered. Everything was lost. My brothers and I had nothing but an absentee mom and no religion. Literally, no religion. But that didn't faze Gloria. She was up to the task. Gloria was a devout Catholic, and as far as she was concerned, it was never too late to get spiritual nourishment.

The first thing she did after we moved in was register my brothers and me into school at the local Catholic Church where her girls attended. Next step, Catechism classes on Saturday mornings. This did not help her popularity. No matter, we were fast tracked from Baptism to First Communion to Confirmation and in no time flat we were full blown Catholics. She put the rest in God's hands.

Gloria tried to teach me to cook. She said it was the most important things a young girl should learn. I fought her tooth and nail.

I said, "Why do I have to learn? Let your daughters cook. They love to cook and they're good at it. What's the big deal? I have other talents. I can iron. I can clean. I can cut the grass, but please, don't make me cook."

She was determined, but so was I. I banged around in the kitchen slamming doors and cabinets. And I cried a lot, too. It was an Academy Award winning performance. When I realized that I wasn't going to win the Gold, and I was in charge of dinner, no ifs ands or buts, a solution to this nightmare began to unfold.

I selected a recipe and went to work. Everywhere the recipe called for a pinch or two of salt, I added a tablespoon or two. During dinner that night everyone agreed that cooking was not my strong suit. That was my first and last time to feed the family. There's nothing better than a happy ending to a bad story. So much for learning the art of cooking!

But I could iron. I realized a sense of accomplishment when ironing. Wrinkles in, wrinkles out – all in the stroke of the hot steamy iron back and forth a few times over a damp garment.

Growing up, we ironed everything. Blouses were sprayed, rolled into a ball, and chilled in the refrigerator for best results. They came out looking fresh and crisp. Sheets weren't the easiest because they contained so much material to work with, but once you got it folded a few times it became manageable, and pillow cases were a snap. The reward; there's nothing like a freshly made bed with ironed pillow cases.

Then came my favorite— Dad's underwear. Iron them flat, fold one side over, iron again, fold one side over. Now you have three panels, iron again. Fold up once, in half and Voilà! Ready for the next pair!

One day, I stood in Gloria's kitchen and watched her as she sat alone on the couch and I ironed. It was something to do, it was familiar. Over the mantle hung five high-school graduation photos, one of them was me.

Dad and Gloria bought this house after the last kid moved out. I was the first to start the trend. Dad always said he didn't want to buy anything nice before that because *we'd just tear it up.* He was probably right. He frequently described us to others as *Hell on Wheels!* The fireplace was a perfect place for him to display his brood … close to the fire.

Once when I stopped by to see Dad just for a quick visit and he was standing in the yard, hose in hand, watering the flowers. It was the funniest thing I had ever seen and I told him so. Dad had never changed a tire, planted a tree or washed a dish in his life, let alone water flowers. I didn't know what had gotten into him. He was not what one would call a handy man, but it was obvious he took a lot of pride in his new home.

Coming here today had not been easy. I spent my whole life hating Gloria. It was my job. I mean, after all, she was not my mother and she never would be. But things had changed, and I needed to talk to her now and tell her something very important.

In the refrigerator there was a stack of sprayed and chilled laundry, all wrapped up individually and tight, absent underwear, ready for the task. So I began to iron. And I ironed and we talked. And I thanked her for all that she had done for me. I told her I was sorry and I told her that I loved her.

Denise Ditto Satterfield graduated from the University of Houston–Downtown, *Magna Cum Laude*, with a degree in Professional Writing. She's been published in her college literary magazine and won First Place in the Creative Writing Contest for her short story, *Summer Breeze*. She and her husband Frank live with their furry companions, Jak Tuff Kat and Junior Bunior a/k/a Boo. They have four grown kids and seven grandkids. For excitement, Denise travels the country on her motorcycle when she's not chillin' at the beach in Port Aransas, Texas.

Like a Forked Radish

Roger Paulding

Solomon stood as best man when Kit and Jenny were married in the spring. As the minister began "Dearly beloved," Solomon swallowed a deep sigh. When the minister asked if each took the other to be his lawfully-wedded partner, Solomon fought back tears. By the time Kit and Jenny were pronounced man and wife, Solomon sat on the front pew, sobbing like a lost child.

Jenny looked at him and could not restrain her disgust. "Mr. Seney, you've ruined my wedding!"

Affected by Jenny's anger, Kit turned red. "You're no fun to have around anymore. Why don't you get out of here? Go live with the Indians!"

Without a word, Solomon left the church, packed his plunder and headed for Challagathawah. The Shawnee village was the only place in the world he had ever been happy. If they would take him in, he would stay, sheltered from the cruel vagaries of civilization.

Hissing Snake, son of the Chief, would not let him do that. "If you live with us you must become an Indian. To be adopted into the tribe, you must run the gantlet and prove yourself worthy to be called warrior."

Why not just fight a wildcat, Solomon thought. At least it would be one to one, not one to a hundred like the gantlet. Hissing Snake treated him like a stranger until he gave in and agreed to run.

"You must go into that line naked as the day you were born. You will wear nothing. Not even moccasins."

Solomon shook his head. He let his face register neither approval nor concern, but he was sure he could not do it. *Fine,* he said to himself, you've lost the two women you loved the most. Now die, like they did. *Just die and let your misery take you to hell.*

The gauntlet entailed two parts, the line and the trail.

The line was a hundred feet long with dozens of Shawnees on each side, outfitted with anything that could be fashioned into a whip or a baton.

The trail wound five miles through the countryside. He would be pursued like hounds after a fox. If they caught him, and they would, the torture would be exquisite, not only leading to ignominy, but death.

He was not sure if he really cared whether he survived but at least he would die trying.

At the start of the line, Solomon slowly removed his deerskin clothing. The women who lined the seven-foot-wide path murmured with the removal of each garment. He assumed they had never seen a white man naked, although his body was not pale. His skin was olive and his body hair was black, what there was of it, a little around his dark nipples, a trace running downward from his navel until it bloomed luxuriously over his pubes. When he uncovered his loins, *ohs* and *ahs* came from the women. He could not help grinning, although he was determined to stay as stone-faced as Hissing Snake.

Suddenly, from the crowd, a short Indian man rushed at Solomon. Screeching like an owl, he butted Solomon in the stomach with his head, knocking his breath from him and sending him flat. As soon as he hit the ground, the Indian straddled him and kicked him in the chin. Then he jumped away and shouted that he had vanquished the enemy.

Solomon started to rise. Three women surrounded him. He tried to keep a stern face, but it vanished as he realized the women intended to examine him. He stood still as a statue. Their hands glided over his skin and their fingernails cut his spine like talons. A hand lifted his testicles and squeezed his scrotum so hard, he flinched. He did not look down to see who it was, and would not have known, except the old squaw cried out, "French are cowards. Eat dirt."

Satisfied, the old women shuffled back to the line. Whooping, hollering and chanting broke the brief solitude until the drums started up. Solomon removed his moccasins, laid them on top of his folded leggings and took a deep breath. He considered running home for Maryland.

On each side of the line were forty Indians and he was the enemy. All white men's sins would be expiated on him. Who could guess what vengeance these people longed for? Did one seek revenge for a white scoundrel who killed his wife or his child? Solomon shuddered with apprehension and feared for a moment that he would throw up. Why do this?—he pondered. Why not give up? Put on his clothes and march home with nary a backward glance. Who would know the difference? *Never tell anyone what a coward he had been.* No one would ask him how he ran the gantlet. Nothing would have to be denied.

As if reading his thoughts, Hissing Snake stared at him, a cold hard look. His friend had already labeled him *coward*. If he quit now, those glacial black eyes would plague him 'til the day of his death. He had to do this. He would do it.

Solomon's resolve caught hold and he prayed that God would empower him to run with pride. Standing solidly tall, he stretched, looked toward the sky, and bowed to the Great Spirit. The beating drums grew louder and louder, impatient for him to start. The young girls taunted him with shrill laughter and vulgar comments. Flying Hawk began a low rumble that grew into a piercing glissando, the long wailing cry of a coyote. The great shrieking chorus joined in, accompanied by the clapping of hands and stomping of feet.

Solomon took off down the line. The switches struck his back, long, thin leathery switches made of willow that stung like the scorpion's bite. He would keep his mind on running. He could hurt later.

Where there had been switches, now there were clubs aimed at him. He dodged them, but ahead, a man tested the weight of a tomahawk in his hand. If that weapon struck his head, it would knock him into the next world. He zigzagged toward the man, jumped at him and kicked him hard in the gut. The man tumbled backwards, a surprised look on his face. Now bolder, Solomon flailed the bellies of two more braves. Several others dropped their weapons and stepped back in fear. Gaining strength from his success, Solomon picked up speed and held his head high.

Someone ran after him.

Someone was close behind.

Heavy breathing pounded on his ears.

The switches stop striking him and fell against each other. Had the second part of the gauntlet already started? The crowd waxed silent. The chants stopped. Like parasitic mistletoe on a tree, deadlocked silence hung in the morning air. He darted his eyes backward.

At his heels, raced Hissing Snake's younger sister, Helema. Except for her moccasins, she was as naked as he.

"Keep running!" Helema cried as she forged ahead, passing him.

Grandmother Earth did not approve of women showing themselves naked to their husbands, much less the entire world. He knew that, and the spectators knew and were shocked by her behavior. They stared silently. No woman had ever run the gauntlet, not to mention, naked as a forked radish, and urging on the beleaguered guest.

Solomon's mind went blank and then was flooded with the meaning of her presence. Helema had chosen him to be her husband. Should that be a surprise? Hadn't she told him when she came to his tent at the age of fifteen that she intended to marry him? He had passed it off as the tender excesses of a young girl. Then the switches pelted him again. The warriors screamed and the women jeered, but the young girls' shrill taunting had stopped. Their choruses turned to songs of encouragement for Helema.

Forgetting his pain, Solomon raced ahead of Helema, kicking at those with the heavy paddles, knocking them from the line to protect her. Gradually, the path broadened. The line moved back. They were there for sport, not to be injured themselves. The older Shawnees seated themselves on the ground, satisfied that Solomon had displayed himself honorably. After that, only a few came close enough to hurt him, and those he forestalled with ready blows of his own. None of that prevented the torturing of his feet by the sharp rocks and stinging grasses, leaving his soles torn and bruised like strips of bacon. Despite all the medication waiting for him, he knew he would hobble for days.

He had a hundred more feet to travel. Then the drums would beat for three minutes, giving him a head-start down the trail before the warriors resumed their pursuit, wailing and chanting like hell's own demons. The trail would make the line seem easy. It ran over creeks and streams, across ditches, through a little ravine, up and down several hills. It had not been coursed to remove rocks or boulders, sticks or cockle burrs that would bite his feet like hungry ants. Stomping away any reptile or wild animals waiting in ambush he had not even considered when a week before, he had surveyed the trace.

There loomed ahead a ravine ten feet wide and thirty feet deep that he would have to jump. He had spent several days practicing, only once falling just before he reached the opposing side. He looked forward to the thrill of successfully navigating it.

Playing the weasel was not outlawed, and under a bush near the beginning of the trail, he extracted the pair of moccasins he had hidden earlier. He put them on. It then became a game between Helema, himself and his pursuers. He leaped across the chasm without problem. But he forgot that Helema had had no practice. Helema started across.

"Start further back!" he yelled. "You're too close. Get a running jump!"

She waved at him, and backed up several feet. She started running again. It did not work. She pitched forward into the center of the ditch and lay prostrate as if she might have broken her foot.

"Helema! Are you all right?"

"Yes, go on. I'm right behind you!"

She struggled to rise and could not. He inched his way down the side of the ravine. By that time, she was sitting up. He helped her up, embracing her for a moment, feeling the transference of strength from her body to his.

"Go!" she said, pushing him away. "They will not hurt me!"

He scaled the ravine and started running again. He was angry now, and ran with vengeance, inspiration coming from Helema's presence, a natural exultation begetting an unnatural strength his pursuers did not enjoy. He had coursed two miles now and had only three more to go when suddenly from the bushes before him, a monster with a wolf's head rose to block his path. Solomon stood unprotected, with only his hands to defend himself.

"Die, fool," cried the voice muffled by the mask atop of its shoulders. The wolf set an arrow to his bow and sent it with a quick, deadly aim straight toward Solomon's naked chest.

Solomon ducked, the arrow flying over his head as he rushed forward to tackle the Indian, grabbing him around the waist and wrestling him to the ground. The Indian tried to free himself, but Solomon's naked body afforded no measure of grasp by his attacker. The skirmish continued for a minute, and then Solomon was on top. He put his knee on the Indian's chest and pressed the wolf down, against the ground. But he had misjudged the strength of his opponent. With a mighty kick against Solomon's kidney, the wolf slammed him painfully to the ground. Solomon rose slowly. The wolf hunkered in front of him, waiting for his next maneuver.

Solomon knew he must attack before the Indian produced a knife or a tomahawk. He rushed forward, threw his arms around the wolf and forced him to the ground again, pinning his arms around the wolf's side with an iron grip. But it was a grip too exhausting to hold for long and the wolf struggled to free himself.

With a blood-curdling scream that frightened even Solomon, Helema threw a rock at the wolf's head. His head caught the brunt of the missile and his opponent fell to the ground, the wolf head flying off. Seemingly unhurt, the warrior vaulted into the air, landed on Helema's back, and tried to rip her hair from her head.

Solomon rushed to clamp his fists around the wolf's neck, he tightened his fingers tightened in a strangle hold. Finally the warrior slipped from his grasp and slid to the ground, his face turning blue.

"We must go before the others catch up," Helema cried.

They sprinted down the trail.

Inside the round house of redemption, wearing only a breech cloth, Solomon sat on a white buffalo skin and smoked a calumet with Hissing Snake and Chief Puckshinewah. The teepee was sealed tight with blankets and skins and in the center, a pit contained hot rocks over which water was poured until steam filled the enclosure, cleansing Solomon's body. Messages to the gods about his bravery and strength flowed through at gap at the top.

Solomon finished the calumet and, slightly dazed, lay prostrate on the sacred pelt. Puckshinewah poured more water over the rocks until steam again filled the tepee. The warm vapors opened his pores, preparing them for an administration of herbs. Hissing Snake took sage and sweet grass and rubbed it over Solomon's body to impart a pleasant fragrance. Solomon inhaled deeply. Like a ghost, Puckshinewah rose and slipped through the opening between the skins of the teepee's entrance, out into the darkness.

Hissing Snake picked up a deerskin pouch and poured a mixture of herbs into his palm. Gently, with great reverence, he sprinkled the sacred potpourri over Solomon's chest. Then he bent over him and rubbed the sweet grasses into the skin with long, powerful strokes. Solomon inhaled deeply and felt a strange new power surge through the tiredness of the gantlet.

Hissing Snake, stone-faced as ever, placed his hands on each side of Solomon's face and spoke huskily.

"*Ouisah*. Good. You are a courageous warrior."

From outside the tent, faint sounds of music streamed into the teepee. The Shawnee warriors encircled the tent, dancing and prancing, singing the sacred song of rebirth for Solomon.

Grandfather of Life who watches from the sky above,
We welcome to our family a brother warrior.
Great strength he shows in his arms and legs
Great spirit he displays for our enemies to see,
Solomon Seney, we make you Shawnee, Shawnee, Shawnee!

As Solomon fell asleep, he realized he no longer envied his brother Jonathan. His dejection over Laura's death had vanished. Fanny had become a sweet, but distant memory.

Helema sat guard in front of the teepee, now fully clothed.

Nesting

Karleen Koen

When I was a younger woman, I collected birds' nests. The collection began when two dear neighbors brought me a branch from a tree on their farm, a branch which had an intact bird's nest in its V. I loved it. And then, seeing that nest displayed, other friends began to give me ones they found, a cardinals' nest from a back deck, a nest before a move to another city, tiny nests built atop a door wreath, a nest in which paper had been used as interweaving.

Once when I was driving in pouring rain, there on the trunk of a parked car was a nest. Once I was sitting under a tree saying a prayer. When I finished, the first thing I saw when I opened my eyes was a nest lying on the ground waiting for me.

I loved those nests with all my heart. Over the years, as I failed one marriage and another failed me, and I clawed my way up out of the debris, I carried them with me.

Not so long ago, I visited a friend's weekend country house. The house was rambling and filled with flower prints on the walls and on the sofas. There was a big kitchen with a big table around which her sons, daughters, their husbands and wives, grandchildren, her forever husband and ancient parents gathered at holidays.

And I thought, this house is her life's nest, a place where her family can gather in one container, and she can count heads and hearts and smile on the new little ones and sit at one end of the table and be proud of what she has created with the man she loves, a genuine nuclear family, no divorces cracking it open.

That's what the nests meant to me, I realized, as I slept in a bedroom of that house, an outward symbol of that which had always eluded me and which I had wanted most of all once upon a time, a marriage held sacred because love was held sacred, the same children by the same father, holidays where all could gather in one place, and I could count my blessings.

The other day, one of the cats knocked a nest to the floor, and I was able to sweep it up and put it in the trash without tears.

My young mothering days are over. My family is splintered. I won't ever have the luxury of looking around a big table at what I have created with the man I created it with. I failed at that particular dream.

And that's ok.

And that's a blessing.

There's Nothing Under the Canoe, Honey

Pamela Fagan Hutchins

My husband Eric and I had scheduled our long-postponed honeymoon for Montana in June, which we were surprised to discover still felt like the dead of winter. (We hail from the Caribbean and Houston, Texas.) Since doing the swim portion of our half ironman triathlon training would not be possible during our two weeks of love in the Great White North, we needed to find an upper-body strength and aerobic substitute. Without taking the weather into account, we decided that canoeing or kayaking would suffice.

So off we traipsed to an adorable bed-and-breakfast near Yellowstone, chosen because the owner advertised healthy, organic food. The beets, quinoa, and cauliflower kugel we were served for breakfast weren't exactly what we'd hoped for, but we felt fantastic, and we were fueled up for the honeymoon and the Half Ironman training alike.

Our "Surprise! We're vegetarian!" B&B sat near a tundra lake. For those of you who have not seen a tundra lake, imagine a beautiful lake in a mountain clearing surrounded by tall evergreens. Picture deer drinking from its crystalline waters, and hear the ducks quacking greetings to each other as they cruise its glassy surface. Smell the pine needles in the air, fresh and earthy.

Well, it's nothing like that.

A tundra lake is in the highlands, no doubt, but the similarity stops there — no trees, no windbreak, no calm surface and no scenery. Instead, it's an ice-chunk-filled, white-capped pit of black water extending straight down to hell, stuck smack dab in the middle of a rock-strewn wasteland. Other than that, it's terrific.

Maybe it was because we were newlyweds, but somehow Eric intuited that I would love nothing more than to canoe this lake in forty-degree weather and thirty-five-mph winds, wearing sixty-seven layers of movement-restricting, water-absorbent clothing. Maybe it was because we were newlyweds, but I somehow assumed that because he knew of my dark water phobia and hatred of the cold (anything below seventy degrees), I was in good hands. My new husband assured me this lake was perfect for tandem canoeing.

So we drove across the barren terrain to the lake. Eric was bouncy. I was unable to make my mouth form words other than "You expect me to get in that @#$%&&*$* canoe on that @#$%&&*$* lake?"

I promise, he is smarter than this will sound. And that I am just as bitchy as I will sound. In my family, we call my behavior being the bell cow, as in "She who wears the bell leads the herd—and takes no shit from other cows."

Eric answered, "Absolutely, honey. It'll be great. Here, help me get the canoe in the water. I'd take it off the car myself, but with that wind, whew, it's like a sail. Careful not to dump it over; it's reallllly cold in there. Not like that, love. Where are you going? Did I say something wrong?"

The only response I gave him was the slam of the car door. Anger gave way to the tears that pricked the corners of my eyes. I stewed in my thoughts. I knew I had to try to canoe. I couldn't quit before I started. We were training. If I didn't do it, Eric wouldn't do it, and that wasn't fair of me.

I got out of the car. Eric was dragging the canoe out of the water and trying to avoid looking like a red flag waving in front of me.

Super-rationally, I asked, "What are you doing?"

He said, "Well, I'm not going to make you do this."

"You're not making me. I'm scared. I hate this. I'll probably fall in and all you'll find is my frozen carcass next summer. But I'm going to do it."

My poor husband.

We paddled around the lake clockwise in the shallows where the waves were lowest, and I fought for breath. I'm not sure if it was the constriction of all the clothing layers or actual hyperventilation, but either way, I panted like a three-hundred-pound marathoner. It would have scared off any animal life within five miles, if you could have heard me over the wind. Suddenly, Eric shot me a wild-eyed look and started paddling furiously toward the center of the lake.

"You're going the wrong way!" I protested.

"I can't hear you," he shouted back.

"Turn around!"

"I can't turn around right now, I'm paddling."

"Eric Hutchins, turn the canoe back toward the shore!"

And as quickly as his mad dash for the deep had started, it stopped. He angled the canoe for the shoreline.

"What in the hell was that all about?" I asked.

"Nothing, love. I just needed to get my heart rate up."

I sensed the lie, but I couldn't prove it. My own heart raced as if I had been the one sprint-paddling. For once, though, I kept my mouth shut.

The waves grew higher. We paddled and paddled for what felt like hours, but made little forward progress against the wicked-cold wind.

"Eric, I really want out of the canoe."

"We're halfway. Hang in there."

"No. I want out right now. I'm scared. We're going to tip over. I can't breathe."

"How about we cut across the middle of lake and shave off some distance? That will get you to the shore faster."

"I WANT TO GO THE NEAREST SHORE RIGHT NOW AND GET OUT OF THE #%$&(&^%#@% CANOE."

Now I really had to get out, because it was the second time I'd called the canoe a bad name, and I knew it would be out to get me.

Eric paddled us to the shore without another word. I'm pretty sure he thought some, but he didn't say them. I got out, almost falling into the water and turning myself into a giant super-absorbent tampon. He turned the canoe back around and continued on without me. This wasn't how I'd pictured it going down, but I knew I had better let him a) work out and b) work *me* out of his system. Looking like the Michelin man, I trudged back around the lake and beat him to the car by only half an hour.

By the time we'd loaded the canoe onto the top of our rental car and hopped in, we were well on our way back to our happy place. Yes, I know I don't deserve him. I don't question it; I just count my blessings.

That night we dined out—did I mention we were starving to death on broccoli and whole-wheat tabbouleh?—to celebrate our marriage. Eric had arranged for flowers to be delivered to our table before we got there. The aroma was scrumptious: cow, cooked cow! Yay! And, of course, the flowers. I looked at Eric's wind-chafed, sunburned face and almost melted from the heat of adoring him. Or maybe it was from the flame of the candle, which I was huddling over to stay warm. What was wrong with the people in this state? Somebody needed to buy Montana a giant heater. We held hands and traded swipes of Chapstick.

He interrupted my moment. "I have a confession to make. And I promise you are really going to think this is funny later."

Uh oh. "Spill it, baby."

"Remember when I paddled us toward the middle of the lake as hard as I could?"

"I'm trying to block the whole experience out of my mind."

"Yeah, well, let me tell you, sweetness, it was about ten times worse for me than you. But do you remember what you said about falling in, yadda yadda, frozen carcass next summer, blah blah?"

I didn't dignify this with an answer, but he didn't need one. "Well, you were in front of me, breathing into your paper bag or whatever, when I looked down, straight down, into the eyes and nostrils of a giant, bloated, frozen, very dead, fully intact, floating ELK CARCASS."

"You're lying."

"I am not. It was so close to the surface that if you hadn't still had those tears in your eyes, there is no way you wouldn't have seen it. You could have touched its head with your hand without even getting your wrist wet."

"No, you did NOT take me out on a lake with giant frozen dead animals floating in it." A macabre version of Alphabits cereal popped into my mind.

"Yes, I did," he said, and he hummed a few bars of Queen's "We are the Champions."

"Oh my God. If I had seen it right then, I would have come unhinged."

"More unhinged. I know. I was terrified you would capsize us and then you would quadruple freak out in the water bumping into that thing. I had to paddle for my life."

He was right. I let him enjoy *his* moment. I'm glad he confessed. But I will never canoe on a tundra lake with Eric again. Even if I got my courage up, he would never invite me. He couldn't have engineered a better moment to make me eager to get back in the pool, though.

Pamela Fagan Hutchins is the author of six nonfiction books and one novel, *Saving Grace*. She is also an employment attorney and human resources professional, and co-founder of a human resources consulting company. She spends her free time hiking, running, bicycling and enjoying the outdoors.

Beginning to Balance

Stephanie Torreno

Mom and I always spent Saturdays together. Our day of having lunch and going shopping, or seeing one of the latest movies, usually with Nana Adele and my sister Cris, started when I was a little girl. We continued this tradition through my teens. Even as I became an adult and Mom and I shared a townhouse, Saturdays felt different. The first day of the weekend became our time to have fun – just the two of us. In college, I knew Mom would always convince me to drop the books, remove myself from the computer, and leave my homework behind for a few hours. These outings were our favorite time with each other.

I still see Mom on Saturdays, but our time together is different now.

My morning begins as my radio wakes me for the day. The bedroom continues to feel strange, yet familiar. Looking around the butter-colored walls, I remember the pictures and the mirror that used to hang on them. The bedroom looks sparse with my twin bed and light wood furniture, compared to the queen-sized bed and larger furniture that occupied more space. I can picture the occasional mornings I used to bolt in the door to greet Mom. Lily, her Bichon Frise, growled at me to protect her territory if I attempted to climb up on the other side of the bed. Now, the room is my territory. In fact, the entire townhouse has been mine for almost a year. Only me, in a two bedroom townhouse.

I dress myself, apply my make-up, and make sure I have everything I need before heading downstairs. As I walk through the tiny hallway, I glimpse one of the pale pink walls in my old bedroom. If I have a few minutes, I may go into the office/guest bedroom and check my email or read the headlines online. Over half of the room sits empty without my daybed or other furniture that once decorated it. My cousin Laurie only sees my huge workstation when she sleeps on the mattress in "her" room during out-of-town visits.

Downstairs, taking the covered cups and breakfast out of the refrigerator, I carefully place what my caregiver prepared for me the previous afternoon on my placemat and eat quickly. I finish packing my tote bag with my lunch, magazines, and candy or other snacks I bring for Mom. I'm typically ready well before my Para transit ride arrives. Once in a while, I'm surprised when the cab or minibus shows up early or on time. Rushing out the door continues to make me nervous, even though I have met my awaiting ride hundreds of times. I usually close the back door just before the automatic lock secures my home.

I hope to arrive at the nursing home before Mom needs to go to lunch. Six days have passed, and I need to see her, talk to her, before I push her wheelchair into the dining room. I quickly tell her what I've been doing and share any tidbits of my life she may find interesting. Although I try to refrain from mentioning anything that may worry her, I'm not too good at it yet. I used to tell Mom everything.

My mom's questions typically come before lunch as well. Aside from "How are you feeling?" I sometimes giggle at, but have grown to appreciate, the questions I think are frequently on her mind.

"Are you taking care of yourself?"

"Have you had any falls lately?"

"Is someone coming to help you tonight?"

"Are you eating?"

That last one reminds me of a funnier version she asked Cris two years earlier when I stayed at my sister's house during one of Mom's first hospitalizations.

"Are you feeding Stephanie?"

"What? Does she think you're starving me?" I asked Cris.

Mom certainly didn't realize our roles were beginning to reverse. None of us did. I began to feel the reversal taking place, but didn't truly understand all it would encompass. I still have immense difficulties in my new role, as Mom struggles with hers. When our mother-daughter roles seemed clearer, Mom most likely had difficulties imagining a time when I could care for myself more easily than she could care for herself, or when I would worry about her as much as, or more than, she worries about me.

Thirty-nine years ago, I doubt my mom thought she would worry about her younger daughter living on her own one day. With one daughter, Cristina, who had just turned four in early April 1973, my parents awaited the birth of their second baby toward the end of the month. When I showed no signs of wanting to come into the world, and with the doctor going on vacation, my mom headed into New York's Bellevue's Maternity Hospital in Niscayuna, New York. She would be induced on April 28th. After a short period of time, labor started, progressed quickly, and Mom delivered me. She did not hear my cry, though. Mom recalled doctors and nurses rushing in and out of the delivery room, as her physician started whacking the seven pound, blue baby on the bottom. As Miss Foley, my favorite teacher in middle school joked with me when she asked about my birth, "You were born a Smurf!" Baby Smurf eventually wailed.

Doctors later told my mom and dad, and Mom explained to me again and again when I became old enough to ask, that I pressed on the umbilical cord as I came down the birth canal. During those few minutes, I was deprived of oxygen, causing damage to the parts of my brain that control movement and speech. My birth would be described in my medical charts as "difficult" and "traumatic." Although I breathed on my own after the whacking, I stayed in the hospital for a few weeks as tests were administered. A spinal tap confirmed that I didn't have bleeding on the brain. Doctors casually informed my parents that I could be blind, have learning disabilities, or not have any impairment at all.

Mom always said I was a fussy infant, crying incessantly when I wouldn't, or couldn't, settle down to sleep. Nana Adele, my maternal grandmother, would tell me how she patiently rocked me to sleep many nights. After a few months, my parents started to notice that my tiny hands were clenched in fists most of the time. My head flopped all around my shoulders. I would startle at the slightest noise in the room. Comparing my development, or lack of it, to my sister's, my mom took me, a year-old child, to the pediatrician, who referred us to a neurologist. Mom remembered that the doctor performed a cursory exam, including throwing a sheet over my head that I didn't make any sudden attempts to pull off.

He then told my mom that I had cerebral palsy.

Mom recalled that moment as one of the loneliest in her life. She had brought me to the appointment by herself. She did not know anything about cerebral palsy – had never even heard of the condition. The neurologist began rattling off information about physical, occupational, and speech therapy. His recommendations included beginning these therapies immediately.

My parents received much more information about my disability in the months and years ahead. CP was the brief and general diagnosis; my official diagnosis read "athetiod cerebral palsy with spastic quadriplegia." Athetiod means that I have a lot of uncontrollable, writhing movements, and quadriplegia involves these movements in both arms and legs. While many individuals with CP are involved on one side of the body, my impairments are unusual in that my right arm and my left leg are weaker and show the most involvement. The spastic part of the diagnosis causes my muscles to tighten, and is more noticeable when I get excited or really nervous. Although I have learned to better control the spasticity, my right wrist aches from the tightness. I continue to have to will my right fist open to grasp an object. When I really need to get a good night's sleep, a muscle relaxant helps me.

I began the triple combination of physical, occupational, and speech therapy soon after my diagnosis. Physical therapists thought I had the ability to walk, so they advised my parents not to put me in a wheelchair. One of the primary goals in my early therapy was to get me on my feet and walking. To accomplish this goal, Mom and Dad followed therapists' advice and let me stay overnight for a few weeks at a rehabilitation hospital. Pictures taken of me in the hospital, holding onto the rungs of a metal crib, show me looking like a caged animal ready to spring from confinement. And that's exactly what I did. I was not going to stay there, away from my mom and dad, for however many weeks they wanted to hold me captive. In about two weeks, I got up and started walking in my royal blue and white sneakers with toddler-sized crutches. Starting to walk ended my captivity.

In addition to outpatient therapy, my parents worked with me at home. Dad encouraged me to walk around outside on the grass, and once I developed better balance, I had great fun trying to strike his leg with one of my crutches! Nana Adele and Daddy George, my grandfather, also helped me practice new activities. Daddy George, who thought of the name when my toddler sister began calling him Daddy a few days after my parents went on a trip, weighted down my Fisher-Price shopping cart so I wouldn't tip it over as I pushed it to walk. He and I also practiced picking up small objects when he and I would shoot marbles down an incline made of books and my Fisher-Price record player! I grasped the multicolored marbles with my whole hand, and not my thumb and index finger that Nana always tried to convince me to use.

While on the floor, I most likely sat in the "w" position, which I was not supposed to do, even though it gave me greater stability. Still, playing with Nana and Daddy George gave me more therapy disguised as fun. Nana also took great pride in claiming to be my first speech therapist when she worked with me on learning how to say "Mom" to surprise her after my parents came home from a trip.

Ongoing PT consisted of lots of balancing exercises and learning how to catch myself before hitting the floor. My favorite one involved lying on my tummy on a huge primary colored ball, rolling around as the therapist held onto me by the legs. I had to hold out my arms and practice pushing back with my hands while holding my head up. This exercise began to engrain the importance of holding my head up when I start to feel like I'm losing my balance. Rolling on the ball made me practice strengthening my muscles and maintaining my balance when I wasn't laughing too hard to practice the goals.

Whatever OT I had, mostly in preschool, didn't seem any fun to me. Exercises to practice manipulating small objects, buttoning oversized buttons, or trying to pull large zippers up and down became extremely frustrating with fingers that didn't want to do any of it. Even grasping food and attempting to get it from hand to mouth didn't encourage me much. To this day, I avoid finger food as much as possible and eat almost everything with a fork. Spoons took more patience to master, but I eventually learned to feed myself cereal and chunky soups as I got older. As I received less and less OT in school, my parents worked with me improving my less than fine motor skills. Mom's experience as an elementary school teacher led her to bring home many handwriting workbooks in which she wanted me to practice forming letters, but they mostly remained blank. My best OT exercises came much later, after high school, when I had to, or wanted to, figure out how to sign my name, apply make-up, or open my own mail.

Speech therapy was the one constant I could count on throughout school. It began as soon as I started talking because I was so difficult to understand. I kept talking, though. The one time I stopped talking happened a year or two after all of my therapy began. I pushed myself so hard to achieve goals in all of my therapies that I shut down and stopped talking. My parents worried that I was regressing. The therapists agreed that my intense motivation to do whatever they wanted me to do was actually causing me to withdraw and stop trying. After a short break, everyone who worked with me eased me back into my routines so that I could continue making progress.

When I became old enough to understand that I had a disability, I saw how different I was from other children. Watching my sister play with friends made me begin to realize what I could not do, even though I was younger than they were. Of course, as I grew up, more encounters with peers would highlight my differences.

I'm guilty of feeling sorry for myself throughout my life. I still have my pity party moments. My feelings would be put into perspective many times, though, as I saw other children with CP who had more impairments than I did. Some would be strapped into reclining wheelchairs, and other kids I saw during PT could only lie on a mat, moaning while a therapist would try to move their spastic arms and legs. And while I saw children with my disability who could do a lot more than I could do, or whose speech could be more easily understood, seeing kids with more severe forms of CP allowed me to begin to realize how indeed lucky I was. Reminders of how differences can affect individuals so greatly, particularly with the same diagnosis or label, would help me keep my balance between accepting my limitations and achieving my possibilities.

Stephanie Torreno lives in Houston and is self-sufficient except for driving a car.

Family, Friends, and Miracles

Lynne C. Gregg

After eight chemotherapy treatments my cancer cells were still growing out of control. I was accepted into a stem cell transplant program. I had to qualify for the program to make sure my body was strong enough to accept all of the harsh chemicals that would be part of the procedure. My tumor markers were growing higher every day. My doctors told me it was urgent that I start the stem cell transplant procedure right away.

My second problem, besides having out of control breast cancer, was that I wanted to travel from Houston to Iowa for my dad's seventy-fifth birthday. Dad had been having heart problems, and I felt an urgent need to see him. I didn't want to admit even to myself, but I thought it might be the last time we saw each other. Both of us had huge health issues. Dad was scheduled to have a procedure to stop and start his heart to try to regulate his rhythm. He could hardly move without losing his breath. I wanted to be with him for the procedure. Fortunately my oncologist reluctantly decided I could make a quick trip to Iowa.

I flew home with my sister Julie who is a nurse. I was a teacher still in the classroom on the days I could make it. We took a late Thursday evening flight so we would have more time to spend with Dad. I had to wear a special mask on the plane and felt as if everyone was staring at me, but my oncologist told my sister, "No mask, no trip."

Julie decided we should surprise Dad and not tell him we were coming. I was worried the surprise would be too much for his heart, but Julie, the medical expert in our family, assured me he'd be fine. Julie had a good friend pick us up at the airport, so Dad wouldn't suspect a thing. We let Mom in our secret trip so she could wait up for us.

We arrived at 1:00 A.M. We tiptoed into Dad's room and started kissing him all over his face and head saying, "Dad, your little girls are home to celebrate your birthday."(I was almost fifty and Julie was thirty-six.) He was a little confused at first, but then he got up and we talked for a couple hours before we all called it a night, or rather a morning!

I only had four days to spend in Iowa before I had to be back in Houston to begin my stem cell transplant. I took advantage of every minute calling friends and relatives and talking with Dad as we sat side-by-side in the living room recliners. I wanted to invite all my friends and relatives over for a hug, but my medical team had advised me against that to minimize my germ exposure.

Mary Kay lives in Iowa. She has been my best friend since we were seven years old. I called her to meet me at this tiny café for breakfast. We did more talking than eating while catching up on each other's lives. I had pictures of my new grandson, and she had pictures of her daughter's wedding. Whenever we see each other, we take up right where we left off, talking non-stop.

All at once Mary Kay got up and walked away from the table. She was coughing into a napkin. I just thought she walked away out of courtesy to me since I was trying to stay completely healthy for my stem cell transplant. I looked over at her when she didn't return to the table. Her face looked purple!

I jumped to my feet and shouted, "Are you okay?" She shook her head trying desperately to gulp in some air. She was choking on something!

I rushed over to her and grabbed her to do the Heimlich maneuver. I was weak from eight rounds of chemo, and my hands broke apart the first time I tried my upward pull. I remember yelling in the tiny eatery, "God, help me. Mary Kay cannot die."

I locked my fingers together in a grip I knew would hold. I belted out some kind of Karate yell, and I pulled upward again with all the force that was in me. A piece of sausage flew from her mouth, and she started to cough and then breathe. Paramedics rushed in the door and proclaimed her okay. She thanked them, but they told her to thank me because I had saved her life. We both thanked the waitress who called 9-1-1. We talked some more, and then it was time to say good-bye. We hugged and took a picture together and then parted "until next time."

Later that same day, Mary Kay stopped back by my parents' house. She had a small sculpture by a local artist of two little girls hugging. She said it represented us when we met and all the hugs she wouldn't be able to give me as I battled cancer far away in Texas.

"You're so strong. I don't think I could be as strong as you," Mary Kay said through tears. "Then *you* have to save *my* life. And you're the one with cancer."

With a grin through *my* tears, I replied, "You would have done the same thing for me—wouldn't you?"

We giggled and hugged and said our second good-bye. Friends for over forty years don't have to say much to know how the other feels.

When I told my parents' minister the story, he just smiled and told me God often uses people to perform his miracles.

Monday morning arrived and my short vacation was almost over. It was 6:15 A.M. and we were at cardiac out-patient surgery with my dad.

First a nurse took Dad's pulse, a strange look came over her face, and she left. When the EKG technician finished his job, the same odd look came over his face. Julie, Mom, and I were all beginning to get nervous as Dad's heart doctor walked in. He reminded me of Barney: purple scrubs, purple hat, and purple high-top basketball shoes.

"Well, Ray, what have you done? Today you have a perfect p-sinus heart rhythm. I see no reason to stop and start a healthy heart."

Dad grinned and pointed at my sister and me. "These two girls are my daughters from Houston. They flew in to surprise me for my birthday. When you turn seventy-five and two women jump into your bed at 1:00 AM, and start kissing you, no matter who they are, strange things happen to your heart."

Dad's surgeon laughed and said, "You girls can take credit for shocking your dad's heart back into perfect rhythm. Congratulations."

My parents' minister was at the hospital with us. He looked at me and smiled. We both knew that it was another miracle.

I flew home to Houston for the third miracle. My stem cell procedure, although very difficult at times, was successful. No sign of any cancer grows in my body. It's been many years since my diagnosis—years full of family, friends, and especially miracles.

Lynne has been writing since she was seven when she began her continuing saga of *Little Delfina*. Her two favorite magazine articles published are: "Angel in Hot Pink Sequins," in *Women's World* and "A Tale of Three Babies" in *Supertwins*. The first about her flashy daughter, Angela, the second about her daughter, Liz, mommy of triplets.

Two Queens Beat a Royal Flush

John W. Hathorn III

'Jealousy' might not be the right word. How about 'double covet'? My objects were twin sisters. Identical twins. The most beautiful twenty-year-old ladies in our two adjacent kingdoms. I knew. I'd toured many lands and had not found any one woman more desirable than these twins.

When me, King Owen Wickham of Bushnell, reached twenty-four, he should have, or be betrothed to, a suitable queen, shouldn't he? Bushnell was adjacent to the Kingdom of Harkmore which was ruled by the parents of the twin princesses Ellen and Elaine Bosworth. Our families attended numerous celebrations,–anniversaries and festivities in each kingdom. During each visit, the twins and I played, danced, rode and sat in court together. We essentially grew up together. I learned never to play dress-up with them because all the discarded clothing at their palace were from women, and they always dressed me as a female. In none of these times together was I able to discern any mark, feature or mannerism that enabled me to tell the difference between them. Much of the twins' time was spent early in life trying to answer who they were to everyone. Getting bored with that, the princesses took to suggesting, "Just call us *Either*." They dressed identically, styled their hair identically and practiced the same phraseology and intonations as though it were a game to blend their personalities.

I fell in love with the composite mixture. Rather than choose one, I wanted both. So what was this, *passion unbridled*?

My announcement of this to my mother, Queen Regent Anna Wickham, almost caused her to grab a pick and chisel Father out of his eternal resting place in the floor of the cathedral. Mother turned every color under the sun, screamed every foul word heard in the lowest sections of the village, and searched the entire Civil Law for some ordinance to prevent me from falling prey to my double dose of lust. After Mother settled down, she said the most logical thing she had voiced since I was crowned. She announced that she was going to visit King Rupert Boswell and his queen, Sophia. They'd arrange my wedding to one *and only one* of the princesses.

Mother packed without any idea of how she was going to select between

Either. Of course, neither did she have any idea how she would identify them, nor which trait would be the deciding factor.

Fearing this weakness in her plan, I accompanied her. She did not speak during the trip–her way of punishing me for causing trouble. To Mother, silence equated to tar and feathering at the diplomatic level.

When we arrived, I renewed acquaintances with my loves, Either. Our mothers went straight to their business. They sent the three of us out and locked themselves with King Rupert in his office. There they spent all day and into the evening discussing and planning.

Whatever agreement the queens hammered out, King Rupert approved it and delivered the plan as a royal ultimatum: in a month, both princesses will visit Lockner Castle in Bushnell and stay for the summer. At the end of the summer, there *will* be a wedding. Three months should be long enough for the three of us to become more closely acquainted–everything short of intimacy. Maybe some decisive mannerism would show itself to favor one or the other Either. At the end of the summer, whichever girl, who is willing, will marry and become Queen Wickham of Bushnell. The other daughter will remain in Ocean View Palace and train to rule as Queen of Harkmore when King Rupert steps down to trade his scepter for a fishing pole.

As Rupert revealed his decision to us, the first part of his proclamation caused expressions of glee on Either's faces, but the latter condition turned the glee to tears and total rejection of the plan.

I was totally taken aback when Either avowed that they did not want to be a queen *anywhere* without me as their king. And Either certainly did not want to have to marry some prince whom they did not love. Then both simultaneously fired off a full broadside by announcing that they loved me, and I was the only man Either could ever love.

I had never realized how deep Either's feelings were toward me. My feelings toward each of them were exactly the same. Even though Either's expressions of their love made me swell with pride, it put the burden of making the selection on me.

"Jealousy?" I could not bear the thought of any other man possessing the one I did not marry. "Double covet?" I wanted both.

When mother and I returned home, we prepared for the Either's arrival. Queen Sophia was also going to stay for the duration. Either did not want to waste our time planning wedding details, they'd let the mothers arrange things. We three felt that our time would be better spent exploring our feelings and emotions. The goal was that this summer's visit should result in my selecting one of them as my queen or one of them rejecting me as her husband.

Initially, Queen Sophia and Either settled in a family apartment in the guest wing of our palace. After three days, Either and I realized that we needed to spend our time as close as possible without parental supervision. Somewhat to our mothers' reluctance, we three took over the visiting family apartment with its three bedrooms. Their two adjacent bedrooms opened into a family sitting room and a third bedroom on the opposite side of the sitting room, which had previously been Queen Sophia's, became mine.

For two days, I respected their privacy, but Either immediately resumed their habit of dressing for bed then invading each other's room to talk, dream, share. They were unimaginably close and shared a base of common knowledge that was uncanny. On the third evening after dressing for bed, Either took to returning to the sitting room to include me in their talks. On the seventh night just as I finished changing, Either invaded my bedroom, sat on my bed and we talked until far after the sentry announced midnight. We eventually fell asleep and did not wake until morning. Just before the maids entered the sitting room to set up breakfast, Either quickly returned to their own bedrooms and faked awakening, fresh and ready for a new day. The ruse did not work because un-mussed bed covers in their rooms became common knowledge throughout the serving staff.

This became a routine. No debauchery ensued since I was reluctant to make advances to one in front of the other. I don't think the sisters were as reluctant to get close as I was since a virgin bride was not a part of their kingdom's Civil Code. In Bushnell I had to wait until our wedding night. Either became more suggestive with the passing of nights, but I quickly changed the subject when it came up.

Two or three weeks went by before I suggested we take a horseback ride on a circuit that passed through both kingdoms. Either had always been impressive equestrians, but I became more amazed at their engineering knowledge of road and bridge construction and, more important, locating them to serve the most citizens. Either as queen would be an invaluable aide to tailoring a capital improvement campaign to serve the most people.

Very quickly, I exposed my heart–my dual chambered heart. I could find no way to divide my love. An act of God would do no good because He had already acted by creating two such perfect queens for me. I needed time to think.

Early one morning, I stole out, saddled my most-spirited Arabian and set out alone on a ride through Bushnell. Challenger's barely-tamed spirit which responded to the subtle controls I gave him, reminded me of my father's teaching: "A king should gather in all the controls at his fingertips when the world is getting out of hand. With the best advice available, only he can make the final decision." The decision was mine and no one else's.

Upon my return, I isolated our two mothers. "Mother, I think I have a solution to selecting between the girls. Either will have to come down the aisle in identical dresses with their faces covered by veils. Both Prince Von Heuben and I will await them at the altar. I will marry one and Heuben will marry the other."

"But which, Owen? Which girl will you marry?" Queen Sophia asked.

"They're both identical in every way. I'll just stand next to one in her veil and start repeating the archbishop's vows. Von Heuben will then say the vows with the other. We'd both get identical prizes."

"But," Queen Sophia said, "neither of my daughters wants Von Heuben. One of them will have a broken heart and grow to hate her sister and you. If she refuses Von Heuben, you don't want to be stuck with a wailing, rejected princess at the altar, do you?"

"All our lives, we royal children have been taught that we may have to sacrifice happiness for the good of our country. For Either, Heuben isn't such a sacrifice; after all, he is *Crown Prince* of Yorkland, remember. He's handsome, smart and athletic. All through University, he did nothing but pester me as to what the Eithers were really like. One of the princesses would become both Queen of Harkmore and Crown Princess of Yorkland. She is going to become a very powerful woman. I don't have that much to offer."

When I described the wedding ceremony to my loves, Either cried. Even though reluctant to agree, they were resigned to their flip-of-the-coin fate being a random choice. By wearing veils, both would be hidden. Both would have an equal chance of becoming my wife.

The remainder of the summer passed far too quickly. The days were filled with events that were made more enjoyable by Either's resolve to appear more fun than the other.

Queen Sophia noted that this was the reason both twins were so accomplished. They always had an attitude of competition, of outperforming her sister, of not being *the other*. The competition only resulted in Either's skills advancing in parallel paths toward being even more identical.

As it approached, I dreaded the scheduled wedding day so I found a few hours alone to make a third plan–one that sated my greed yet seemed to conform to the expected. The season of dual fun would end, and my camouflaged scheme could only unfold at the altar.

After Either, with some trepidation, accepted the "husband by chance, not choice," they loosened up and returned to the fun we had always enjoyed. The un-chaperoned closeness provided many opportunities for Either to pull the practical jokes and mischief I had experienced in our growing years. One supper my wine goblet was filled with red ink. One morning after we had breakfast and gone into the city, the maids came to clean my room only to find the princesses' stockings, underskirts, chemises and bloomers strewn over my bed and furniture and hanging from the chandelier. The stodgy old maids fell for the prank and swiftly carried the news back to our mothers. Fortunately, Queen Sophia knew her daughters well enough to not fall for their mischief. All their stunts did not top the morning I awoke with Either perched on my bed dressed for our day's planned outing, eager for me to arise and join them . . . but I was naked. They had gently removed my nightshirt while I slept. To make matters worse, they would not take their weight off the covers so I could wrap myself in the sheet. They thrilled watching me slide toward the headboard and sandwich my privates between two pillows to escape to my dressing room.

The only time we were separated was when Either had to attend fittings of their identical wedding dresses–which I was not allowed to see. The mothers insisted the dresses be exactly the same, no feature of one dress could draw more attention than the other. Either had to appear identical to assure that my choice was unbiased.

These efforts were successful because both brides came down the aisle on either arm of King Boswell, looking as though a mirror reflected the image of one bride onto his other arm. This uniformity extended to the bouquet each carried.

King Boswell marched Either to the altar, paused, stepped back and said, "Queen Sophia and I willingly offer our daughters to this union."

The Archbishop asked, "Princesses Boswell, do you willingly accept the conditions of this ceremony?"

"I do," came from voices under the veils.

At this moment my secret, self-placating scheme went into effect. The Queen Mothers were probably thinking that the daughters were agreeing to abide by the random selection. No one except Either and I were ready for their answers to the next question.

I stepped between the two brides as the Archbishop asked, "Princess Boswell, do you accept King Owen Wickham to be your husband, to love, honor and obey him until death do you part?"

"I do," came from voices under *each* veil. Giggling followed.

Immediately murmurs began. "What did they say? Did they both say, 'I do?'" The murmurs grew in volume until they filled the cathedral. They drowned out the remainder of the vows–the ones in which I promised to love them both.

Prince von Heuben turned to face the queen mothers with a sickly smile, gave them a shrug and stepped down from the altar step.

As our "I do's" were sinking in, I hurriedly slipped two identical rings on the two identical hands that were proffered from under the two identical veils.

My mother slid forward in her pew and grabbed the pew back in front of her before she slipped all the way to the floor.

Queen Sophia cried out, "No! No! No! You've done it all wrong. You're supposed to select <u>one</u> of my daughters."

We ignored both her vocal and whispered protesting and continued with the ceremony. Within the next five minutes, I had taken both my loves to wife, and we were on our way back up the aisle.

Before we were allowed to enter the palace ballroom for the reception, Queen Sophia and my mother steered us to a private room for an accounting. Queen Sophia reprimanded me harshly. "You did this. You are responsible for this disgrace. Even my mischievous daughters could never think up such a terrible joke. This wedding is going to be annulled before you ever go to your adulterous wedding bed. My daughters are not whores that you can have with no consequences. You will not enjoy a ribald threesome with my daughters, young man."

"Please, Mother," Either said, "we want this. Neither of us could step aside at the altar so we decided to share Owen. Remember, you taught us to share everything else. You didn't say, 'except a husband.'"

"Owen?" My mother was scowling. "This is no way to start your reign.

What kind of example is this going to set for the people?"

Mother made sense, but to reverse our action would put us right back to steering our ship back into the storm. I asked them, "Well, Either, do you want to make a choice now?"

Either must have been thinking of a compromise and offered it. "Okay, Mother, if you won't shame us at the reception, we'll go to our wedding chamber and the one who emerges still a virgin in the morning will step back, agree to an annulment and marry Prince Von Heuben."

I could not erase my experiences when, in times past, Either simultaneously shared the same thoughts. One had something on her mind and the other perceived what it was. Either had displayed the same look as when they had set up a joke and were waiting to see someone fall victim.

I expected the reception and celebrating to last until sunrise; however, we three stole away and retired to our own private party in our sitting room. After a toast with a special bottle of champagne I had secreted away for the occasion, the twins summoned their dressers to change from their wedding dresses and left me. Both returned in very revealing nightgowns.

After emptying the champagne with a couple more toasts, I was told to go to my dressing room and prepare to visit one of them. In the meantime Either would each retire to one of the two bedrooms–not necessarily the bedroom Either had occupied these last three months. I was not to know which bride awaited me behind which door. I'd randomly enter a bedroom and consummate the marriage with one of my loves.

This plan would have worked had my first-chosen, first-consummated wife not remembered that her mother had advised the daughters that a wife should not sleep all night with her husband. She should insist that she be granted her own apartment and he be invited to visit her bed, make love, and return to his after. Supposedly, this was the only way a wife could assume control of their intimacy and maintain her privacy.

After our initial lovemaking, I reluctantly retired to my bed but could not quell my enthusiasm enough to fall asleep. Thus, I endeavored to return to the bed of my bride; however, in the dark and in my excitement to cuddle in her warmth, I must not have returned to the same princess's bedroom I had entered originally.

My bride did not sleep but eagerly welcomed me into her arms. As our embraces advanced to the union, my mistake became immediately apparent.

This was not the second time with my first bride, but the first time with the second bride. Both love-makings had been initiated with a slight cry of pain.

As soon as my second bride had enough and giggled herself to sleep, I stealthily returned to my bed. This time, the "long" walk back to my bed seemed like a trek across the kingdom. I lapsed into a very deep slumber, only to be awakened by my two beaming brides out-shining the beaming morning sun as it flooded the room.

Both thanked me for choosing her to consummate our marriage. As they voiced this thanks, they gave each other a puzzled look. Had I slept with them both? If so, which one was first?

We had not heard the sentry call the hour, thus neither of us knew the hour I visited Either. And since both woke and came to wake me, I could not verify which bride was in the bedroom I exited last. Apparently my camouflaged scheme to marry both princesses had succeeded in spite of our belated attempt to unravel the dual vows.

One bit of unmistakable evidence of what had happened that night was present. Both beds' sheets showed where two virginities had been forfeited to love.

The princesses' puzzled looks were reshaped into smiles that eventually emitted two side-splitting laughs. Either, bonding through their mental connection, lifted the hems of their nightgowns over their heads and threw them in the air. Their identical bare bodies wriggled down under the covers and pressed next to mine. With arms wrapping me in a cozy tangle of elbows and hands, their legs captured my thighs in strong vice grips.

A feeling of joy and pleasure overcame me as I realized that my blundering scheme had such an agreeable outcome. Rather than being torn apart by the possessiveness of two women, I was being pressed together between two sharing sisters. I was to share my body, my love and my kingdom with my two prizes. I had captured the sun, moon and all the stars in the galaxy.

Rather than a mutual lovemaking which would surely embarrass the other bride, we laid enfolded, tickling and giggling. When I began to map out roads over the hills and valleys of our two kingdoms on the sheet covering their nude bodies, we migrated into a discussion of the dispensation of our two kingdoms. "Rather than one of us remaining in Harkmore and become its queen as father wants," One Either said, "we should merge the two kingdoms and control them from Lockner Palace in Bushnell. It is centrally located in the two territories. Either can bring the people of Harkmore over and bind them to the unified kingdom."

"Father is looking to retire from the king business," the other Either said. "Surely he'll agree to a merger as soon as we work out the laws and other details."

While the signed paper combining the kingdoms was being waved and shown to the people by the two Dowager Queens, King Rupert, having had a bit too much wine, retreated unsteadily into the throne room of his castle.

Rupert turned and drew his sword and said, "Gone is Rupert's justice. Gone are Rupert's laws." He pointed the tip of his sword at his pet bloodhound and said, "But gone you are not, Sir Ditherworthy, yet I'll no longer need your barking advice since I now sit the throne one last time."

Rupert looked at the dog and motioned him to come. The aged bloodhound slunk up to the throne and placed his chin on the king's knee. Rupert patted the dog's head then ran his finger down the full length of Ditherworthy's characteristic nose. "You're the only one, Sir Ditherworthy. Your nose is the only way I could ever tell the difference between my two daughters. I could always send you to fetch a specific one, and you never failed to bring just that one back to me. You're the only one who could possibly unscramble this mishmash, the only one who knows which is Ellen, the first born, the rightful heir. Neither of my tricky little misses is willing to admit the identity that only you know, which Either is Either." Rupert shrugged with resolve, "No reason undoing a spicy stew that will satiate so many appetites for gossip. Sir Ditherworthy, let's go fishing tomorrow morning, bright and early."

John Hathorn is a long time member of the Houston Writers Guild. In a former life, he was a meteorologist and owned his own company. He lives in Houston with his wife Lil. They have four children and one grandchild.

Ends and Beginnings

Sandra Morton

Sunday, November 28, 2004, 10:00 PM
Monday, November 29, 2004, 4:40 PM

I went to bed wearing shoes, socks, sweats and rainbows. My motorcycle helmet and duct tape lay on the bedside dresser. I didn't have to wear them at night.

I'd like to think I knew when I went to bed that night, it would be the last time I'd have to sleep fully clothed, the last night I'd sleep with one eye open, the last night I'd listen for the television in the living room to go off, signaling that my husband was coming to bed. I wouldn't have to wear the helmet to prevent brain damage when he pounded my head. No duct tape to keep me from accidently speaking when he was watching television. But I wasn't thinking that far ahead. It was another night of questions. Would he turn on the overhead light, hoping to wake me? Would he waken me to carp about my shortcomings, knowing I had to work the next day? Would he want me to get out of bed to go outside to the barn or garage to turn off the lights *he* forgot? Would it be a new torture I hadn't dreamed of yet? None of the above. He crawled his nasty, naked self into bed.

I lay awake a long time, and I was still awake several hours later when he got up to forage and watch more TV because he couldn't sleep. I must have slept because 5:00 AM came much too soon.

He was snoring in bed when I rose to make coffee and get things set up for him when he decided to get up. Then I went to the restroom to face myself in the mirror. He had never marked me so badly all over, but he'd used the whole week of Thanksgiving to wreak havoc on my body. My face wore green, yellow, purple, and charcoal—and that was just my face. I could cover the rest of bruises and scratches with clothing, but no makeup artist alive could have done justice to my face.

I had two alternatives. I could go to work and lie about my injuries, or I could stay at home and never heal. Lying won.

I arrived at work way earlier than usual so I wouldn't have to see my colleagues. They would ask, I would lie, they would disbelieve. I was so wrecked that no lie would be believed, so I'd stay out of everyone's way. I ran into one of my principals near my classroom, so I steered him to my "good" side. I pretended that he didn't see the damage, and he pretended he didn't see.

The students were a different story. Junior high students are nosy. All teachers have to be actors, and I was an Oscar contender that day.

"Miss, what happened to your face?"

"I was in an accident."

"Oh, Miss, were you driving? Were you in your car?"

"No, a friend was driving an old Ford pickup, and my seatbelt broke when my friend stomped on the brakes to avoid rear-ending someone. I hit the dashboard with my face."

"Wow, you sure got a lot of colors on your face. Did you get hurt anywhere else?"

"Yes, I have an ugly bruise where the seatbelt was before it broke."

And so the lie went. Students who weren't in my class stopped by my room to see the Rainbow Lady. I didn't tell them about the lumps on my skull, the claw hammer scratches on my back that were partially healed already. I certainly didn't mention the purple/black bruise on my pubic bone where the end of a 2x4x8 foot board was rammed into me with the warning to "put that little dick back in, you bitch!" I earned that for moving the board a half inch too far when I was helping build a porch. I didn't yet know about the broken nose that would soon need surgery.

That Monday flew by fast, meaning the eight hour respite from hell was over. Weight pressed on me with nearly three hundred pounds of rage, fear, and grief. Following established procedure, I called home as soon as I could get to a phone without being seen. I had no cell phone at the time. Routine dictated that I call home to see if I needed to stop by a store for groceries.

The answering machine came on. That could mean several things. My husband was too lazy to answer the phone, he was gone, or he was being a giant hemorrhoid. My state of mind wouldn't accept anything logical. No answer felt menacing to me, like he was lying in wait. The jovial message on the phone didn't sound like an abuser. "We're not home right now. I'm out back making pasta for the catfish, and she's outside making rigatoni for the chickens. Just leave a message" I left a message saying I'd be home in twenty minutes.

The weight on my chest became heavier and heavier as I drove the fifteen miles home. I hurt. I was looking at the end of my life. This was my conviction. I'd left him twice before and come back. *Why can't I leave him now? Because I can't, I just can't. Why in the name of pluperfect hell can't I?*

The pressure in my chest increased with each mile, and the blood was pounding in my ears. I was two and a half miles from an evil, living hell. *Maybe I could turn down that Farm to Market Road and keep driving. And go where? Somewhere, anywhere! I can't! I can't!*

I did. One point seven miles before hell, I took a left turn. I drove about a hundred yards, telling myself I could turn back, I wouldn't be too late. *Turn back to what? Probable death? Hell on earth? HELL, NO!*

At that moment, Someone Else pressed on my knuckle-white hands on the steering wheel. Someone Else's foot pushed my foot down on the accelerator. I told myself a few miles later that I could still turn back. Someone Else wouldn't let me. Thank God.

Someone Else took charge to help end my thirty-three and a half year nightmare. At 4:40 PM that evening, I declared my independence and headed for the sheriff's department to put matters into their hands. A few hours and many photographs later, I went off in private to mourn and lick my wounds.

Mercy

Kevin Brolan

Sister Marion Patrick is dead. I checked the website for the Dominican Sisters. She died in 02. I had her in the fifth grade. I remember her being very tall. I was ten. She had the face of an Irish cop. She could keep order in a classroom. This is not a maudlin story of abuse. There is no lawsuit in the hopper. The Dominican Sisters did more for me than they ever did to me. By the time we graduated we could all read write and do simple arithmetic in our heads without paper and pencil. We were not permitted to count on our fingers. By the third grade we knew who could stand up to an interrogation and not give up his friends. One of the reasons the NYPD has been so successful in the interview rooms over the years is that historically most of the detectives were products of the Catholic School system. I've never read that theory in a criminology text but I'll stand by it.

What possessed me to do a web search on dead nuns I can't explain. I'm a detective by trade and gathering information for me is natural, like a Labrador retriever looking up, or a hound sniffing the ground. Even wasting city time I'm looking into something. It was my first grade teacher, Sister Catherine who motivated the inquest. She called me "Kevin darlin'" and sent me on errands. She had me open and close the top windows with the long wooden window pole. She was very young and what showed of her face beneath the habit was very pretty. I confess. I was a teachers' pet. I went to the website to see if she was still above ground or maybe see her picture. She is still with us, but no picture.

Then I saw Sister Marion listed among the departed. The mental movies took me back to the fifth grade. The pastor, Father Morrow visited our classroom a half hour before lunch to give a talk to encourage vocations. He tried to sell us on the merits of the boys entering the priesthood and the girls becoming nuns. Father Morrow was a mystical figure to us. He was in his sixties and his glasses were so thick they magnified his blue eyes. They seemed to fill the lens. He said the eight o'clock mass every day but we never saw him any other time. He stood in the front of our classroom and made an animated case for devoting our lives to the service of others and the Church. His voice boomed. His fists clenched and his eyes looked like they'd pop the lenses out of his frames. Then he was gone and we stood up from our wooden desks to file into the coatroom behind the front wall of the classroom.

When I turned the corner into the shadowy closet, out of view of the good sister, I began my imitation of the pastor. "Be a priest! Be a priest! Father Morrow says be a priest!" I widened my eyes and shook my fists as I walked through the long narrow closet. My classmates giggled. Then it got quiet. The first blow glanced off the back of my head. The second landed solid. It was a fist. She called my name as she threw another combination. I crouched and ran out the far door into the front of the room. We faced each other and she jabbed with her left. I got under it. Then she threw a hook with the same hand and caught me high on the head. Then she lowered her hands. I straightened up. We stood there looking at each other.

"Perhaps you'd like to do your little show over in the rectory for Father Morrow."

My stomach knotted in fear of her proposal. My knees felt a little unsteady. My head stung beneath my scalp from the hook. She motioned with her vaunted left like she was swatting a fly and dismissed me. I turned and faced my classmates with a wide smile on my face. I was the main event of the morning.

We received the sacrament of confirmation in the fifth grade. That entails religious instruction in preparation for the visit of the Bishop who performs the Confirmation of the Faith. The Bishop administers a light slap to the cheek of each kneeling candidate as a symbol of willingness to suffer for the faith. The three fifth grade classes were brought over to the empty church for rehearsal of the choreography of the event. Each class occupied assigned pews and proceeded to the altar in designated order. Sister Marion played the part of the Bishop. She was seated in the center of the altar. As the other classes rehearsed in order, her class waited in the second half of the dimly lit church.

Ginch produced a sock puppet from the pocket of his suit jacket. It had eyes, ears and a red ball for a nose. He pulled it over his right hand. It looked to the left and then to the right. Then it bit me on my left thigh. I let out a snort. My shoulders shook silently as I held my breath to stifle a belly laugh. I thought I saw our Sister look our way but wasn't sure. It was pretty dark and we were a good twenty yards from the altar. As we filed out a little later I followed Ginch. We were the last two in the boys' line. Whenever we travelled in a group we lined up by height. Me and Ginch were tall and skinny. We travelled up the center aisle of the church toward the front. I was last in line. The puppeteer knelt down on the thick carpet and received his cursory love tap as I stood behind him. He arose and I knelt in front of the sister with my hands clasped together in prayer. My eyes were closed. I was looking like a little cherub as instructed. Wham! I felt the smack burn into my face as I heard it echo through the church. It sounded like a whip crack. I listed to my left and my hands shot out to maintain my balance. I didn't fall over. Sisters' eyes were smiling. She never said a word about it.

We had a math test. Fifty questions were worth two points each. I got a seventy eight. I got eleven wrong. Sister Marion was not happy with the results. She reviewed each question. After going through the problem everyone that got it wrong had to come up to the front of the room. She used a pointer. It was light wood with a rubber tip that made no noise when it touched the blackboard. You got two whacks behind the legs for every question you got wrong. The girls got it too. I remember hearing it whistle through the air before it made contact. I don't remember it hurting too much. I don't even remember us talking about it. Maybe we wrote it off as a cost of doing business, a little suffering for the faith.

I didn't mention it when I went home. I was changing out of my school pants to put on jeans when my mother passed the open door to my room.

"What happened to the back of your legs?" There were welts. I told her why. Her countenance hardened. She looked like she was watching the British burn her barn. She disappeared into her bedroom and came out in different clothes. "You stay here." is all she said. Her steel grey eyes told me where she was going.

I don't know what the five foot of fury that was my mother said or did at that convent. I don't know how many parents knew. Sister Marion Patrick was giving out key chains and holy pictures the next day. Nobody got hit.

Internal Bleeding

Kevin Brolan

Nobody ever gets over a divorce. "What doesn't kill me makes me stronger." is for prison movies. On paper it wasn't much. No police reports. No money. I got out with ten grand, a Mustang and my clothes. She had some stock I wasn't supposed to know about. I didn't bring it up. I didn't want the house.

My first candidate for a lawyer was an ex-boxer out of LSU, George Peyton. In his last fight he had boxed Willie Pastrano who went on to the Light Heavyweight Championship of the world.

"Go to the bank and take out all the money."

"I don't want it to get shitty."

"It'll get shitty. Trust me. Go get the money."

The lawyer I did use was Murray Lieberman. He was a transplant from the Bronx. Dapper with salt and pepper hair combed back, he sat behind a glass topped desk. "Sue the Bastards" was in gold on a highly polished wood triangle where you would expect a name plate. Murray was my voice of reason.

"Kid, you're trying to make the best out of a bad situation."

I called him from the daycare at the Lutheran school. I was not authorized to pick up my own son. But her live-in boyfriend was. The decree said I got him first and third Fridays at five pm. My son was right there, and I was told I couldn't take him.

"He's my son. It's my weekend. I'm taking him." I said to the blonde young lady behind the desk. She started crying, as if on cue. She wiped a tear with a high gloss blood red nail.

"Get out! I'll call the police!" The booming voice came from behind me. It was the director. He was agitated, standing there like an aged linebacker.

"Good. Get someone over here with some sense. Call the cops."

I waited. The whole concept of other people standing between me and my four year old was hard to digest. I'm picking up my son, from strangers, and the cops are coming. The cops came. They were not excited. The Ex showed up. The boyfriend showed up. They kept their distance like I was radioactive.

"She won't authorize you to pick him up at the daycare. She wants you to pick him up at the house."

The cop's voice had the exhaustion of a veteran of multiple divorces.

"What about now?"

"You have to go to the house."

"But we're all here."

"It doesn't have to make sense. Go to the house."

"Got it."

Divorce wrought new emotional landscapes. I felt backed in a corner. I had to behave or I couldn't see my kid. Yet murder of my tormentor seemed my only out. I had visions of an old friend from the neighborhood pushing her in front of a subway train.

This impulse hung on awhile until I looked in my sons' eyes one weekend and knew I could never hurt his mother.

The biggest fear was that she would move and take the boy. She could go back to Wall Street with a phone call. I was tied to Houston. Firemen don't travel on business. I was the first in my family to divorce. We were New York Irish that stayed married.

When she told me the third time we had to separate I got out without protest.

I went to a priest. I gave him a run down. He said; "Take charge of your own life. Divorce her."

I called my father; "How many times are you gonna do this? Divorce her ass!"

He never liked her anyway.

I tried to figure it out. I quit drinking. I got a real job. She left. Everybody loves a fireman. Well almost.

She was the one thing I took for granted. I never thought she'd leave me. She'd bored into my life like a tick. She encouraged my dreams and never complained about drinking. She never nagged. Maybe she never gave a shit. Anyway, I had to go.

I was always faithful. Well, usually. I got caught once. It was St. Patrick's Day. We had just moved to Houston that Labor Day. I was in Griffs' drinking heavily. Met a girl with black hair parted down the middle. It reached past her belt in the back and caressed the ass of her jeans. She wore a faded denim shirt that covered the mother of all tits. I'd have followed her into hell that night. As it was I followed her behind the VFW hall. Semper Fi.

I returned home about four am and took a shower. The fact that the bars close at two in Houston had slipped my mind. The name and number of my indiscretion was to be ever washed away into the sewer system and I would never do it again. I stood over the toilet and let the 'relationship' go. It missed. The scribbled evidence fluttered to the floor between the bowl and the sink.

The next morning, the words "Get out." rang in my hangover. I opened one eye and saw the barrel of my .44 Special. It seemed a lot bigger looking into it. Her green eyes were bright and watery behind the sights.

"Get out." Not louder but calmer with more of a West Side New Yawk accent. My right hand was wrapped around a pillow under me. I thought I could get the gun from her with my left. But what then? I knew she had the genetics to mess up the headboard. Her maiden name was Kelly.

I never admitted it. I said the name on the paper she found by the toilet was a woman trying to organize a rugby team. I said I wanted to play. It was a passing idea fueled by alcohol and a lie that would fly if she wanted it to.

Maybe she just got tired of me. Was it postpartum depression or no partum depression?

She flew to New York on business again. She took the sheer see through blouse I'd bought her that she'd left unopened.

A wise old man advised me, holding his hand up. "You got a relationship, you got this." His two fingers pointed up. "You got a separation, you got this." His middle finger stood alone.

After reading books and listening to gurus, that's the only relationship advice that stuck with me.

I stumbled through dates. They subtly spoke of their traumas like a short parade of broken toys. They took me places I'd never think to go. Our chemistry intensified the loneliness.

Then I met the nurse running Memorial Park. Bright blue eyes and blonde braids crowned her tanned symmetry. We had sex like workout partners, sometimes laughing after climax like kids who stole something. In six weeks she was marrying a lawyer in Boston. She was soap opera perfect.

Responding to a false alarm in an office building, I met the green eyed, auburn haired legal secretary with the four year old out of THE EXORCIST. Our first date took us to the zoo. "Look at their dicks." He said in the hoarse voice of a fifty year old steel worker, as a giraffe peed. I tousled his fine red hair looking for the horns. My son liked him. Little Red almost ran me off. His mother was love and positive energy in a six foot package. She was the undefined notion of the woman I subconsciously always thought I deserved. I used to drop her off at work downtown just to watch her walk away, high heels clicking, her sculpted hips hugged by a tight skirt. The peace in her eyes and love without strings made me feel different. I felt joy again.

My son told his mother about his new friend and apparently daddy's new friend too. Two weeks later on a Saturday morning my first born comes into the bedroom of my apartment, "Dad, the police mailman is at the door."

It was a constable in uniform and gun belt, serving me with a petition to amend the divorce decree and a summons to Family Court. When Dad's new friend showed up in court and turned heads I saw the eyes that looked over the gun once again. They whispered "This isn't over."

Next Friday when I went to pick him up she wouldn't open the door. Said he was sick. He was crying inside the house. I've kicked through many doors on the job, to make rescues. I looked at the knob and the doorjamb. My right foot twitched. The anger was winning. I was right. Reason said, "Court Order." She wants an incident to document the violence in your heart.

I left, alone, my son's unanswered cries branded into my heart.

It didn't end with SWAT and a news crew. The hostage situation is internal. Her clothes still hang in the closets of my mind.

My first son doesn't speak to me.

Hold Tight the Reins!

Lena Vidrine Roach

"For a pretty girl, you don't look so good," Mom said.

Years ago, those words would cajole in a soft and playful way to get me to open up about a teenage problem. Tonight her tone was nervous and high-pitched. She blinked away as if she didn't expect an answer.

Caught up in what had become a family tragedy, I didn't know how to handle it. The truth was I felt like a traitor. Mom had just been admitted into a nursing home. My two brothers, two sisters, and I had promised to honor her wishes and never let that happen.

Yet here we were, gathered around her bed.

Mom, 83, was once a tireless worker in her vegetable garden and loved to entertain family and friends with her famous Cajun gumbos. Now she was too feeble to attend to some of her simplest needs, yet she refused to live with her children. We hired the best caregivers we could find to help her stay in her home, but no arrangement seemed to work out well.

"She's not eating properly, and she's not taking her medication as prescribed," her doctor warned. "She should be in a good nursing facility."

When Mom heard what he had said, she wiped tears from her eyes. "I never want to leave my home. It would break my heart."

Wanting to comfort her, I wrapped my arms around her, assured her that we loved her and would never take her anywhere against her will.

Now I thought back over the past few days, trying to figure out this unexpected turn of events. She had asked one of my sisters to take her to see her doctor. We were astonished. For months she had refused a checkup. She knew he would bring up the nursing home issue again. Yet silence from her.

Now here she was, in a place she had always said she wanted to avoid. She looked small and frail. Her face was drained, her dark eyes confused. Her lips parted as if she wanted to talk. Ask to go home? Say we had betrayed her?

"Don't worry. She'll be fine," a nurse's aide said. "She's everybody's idea of a loving grandmother." She smoothed the fluffy halo of silver around Mom's forehead and then stepped aside to give us room nearer the bed.

My oldest sister sighed and lowered the rail. Mom gripped her hand and looked around the room. "The walls are a pretty blue, don't you think?" she said, her voice tremulous. "Soft and peaceful."

A numb sense of defeat washed over me. "Face reality," her doctor had said. 'Reality', that double-edged word. A happy truth, or like now, a bitter pill.

Her grandson held the family Bible. He knelt by her bedside, opened the book and held it with one hand, the other gently clasping hers. He began to read, "What time I am afraid . . ."

Mom became agitated. "No, no, no." She shook her head from side to side on the pillow.

A new lump stuck in my throat. My youngest brother whispered, "She won't stay here."

It occurred to me she thought she was getting the last sacrament and that was why she was upset. I wanted to put a hand on my nephew's shoulder and urge him to stop. But suddenly, she smiled, pulled him to her and hugged him.

Memory rushed to an incident when I was five. She and I were on a ride in an antique buggy left by her parents. The country lane was shadowed by towering oaks and sycamores, the rays from a bright ball of sun splintering between their branches.

Mom was a perpetual whistler. That day no songbird could outdo her. The lilting sounds she made were gentle in the woodsy quiet, whether she whistled "Tis So Sweet to Trust in Jesus," her favorite hymn, or the Cajun waltz tune, "Jolie Blonde."

She stopped whistling. "Would you like to take the reins and drive the horse?" she asked.

Thrilled with the idea but intimidated by the huge, powerful animal, I pulled back and shook my head.

"Go on," she said. "You can do it!"

I took the reins, but they were too loose in my childish hands. The horse veered.

"You have to hold tight the reins. You're in charge," Mom said.

Learning had never been so exhilarating. My mind filed away the victory chant, "Hold tight the reins. You're in charge!" The words became a maxim that has seen me through many difficult times in my life.

I remembered other occasions when she spoke of courage to do what one must. After the death of her youngest sister, she'd said, "Some things in life are so hard to accept, they're easy. You have no choice."

Last week she had looked out the window at the lawn surrounding the oak tree she'd planted years ago, a pink blush of blossoms decorating its base. "Just a glimpse of the yard gives me joy," she said. "This place, this family home has always been my castle." Then, a deep sigh and she added, "Life is made up of two *whens*—when to hold on and when to let go."

Mom still wanted to hold on. I just knew it. But here, in a nursing home?

My sister kissed her goodnight. Next, my turn. I tried to be cheerful and casual, the way I'd be if we were in her home.

Later, sitting in my car with the engine idling, I thought of tonight's empty room in the ancestral nest. I didn't feel like a loving daughter who had promised her mother she'd never have to leave her home. I had let her down. All of us had.

Childhood memories crowded my mind. Mom's hand on my forehead when I had malaria. The blackberry pie she baked each year for my birthday treat. I saw her dancing in the kitchen to "Isle of Capri," eyes closed, hands raised around an imaginary partner. When Dad entered, she stopped, laughed and said she'd been "poking a little fun" at her youngest sister. In her flushed face I sensed a kind of abandon she craved.

I looked at a sky full of stars and wondered how Dad would have felt about what happened tonight. "Take care of your mother when I'm gone," he'd said.

I turned off the motor. I couldn't do it—let her stay here. Somehow we, her children, would have to find a way to keep our promise to her. I'd go back inside and spend the night with her. Tomorrow I would take her home.

Tears came fast as I fumbled to open the door. A sudden memory stopped me, and my hand froze on the latch. My eyes focused hard on the corner of the building that was Mom's new address. No more than a month ago, she's said, her tone reflectively quiet, "Nobody should let others make life-changing decisions for them."

My thoughts ran back to that buggy ride with her years ago when I was afraid to take the reins in my own hands and drive the horse. Her other words played back and forth in my mind. It was then I knew how she happened to be in that nursing home. We hadn't put her there. She had done that herself by asking to see her doctor again.

My shoulders lifted. Mom was "holding the reins tight" to keep on taking charge of her life. I had to let her go.

Lena Roach is a Louisiana native and retired English teacher. Her first poem, *Success*, appeared in *Young People's Magazine*, Philadelphia, PA. Other poems appeared in *Kansas City Poetry Magazine, Scribbler's Script, Swamplily Review*, and *Oasis*, a book. Several poems appeared in professional periodicals. She wrote a "Dear Teacher" column for several newspapers, and her articles have appeared in *The Times Picayune*, and the *Lake Charles' American Press*. One short story sold to *GLAMOUR*, England. At present, she is working on a novel.

The Coin

B. Lynn

Once you gave me
The side of the coin you show her—
Focusing, listening, engaging,
Sneaking off
To grow together as lovers.
Now making plans, stealing time
From me,
From us.

Returning home
You offer me your other side:
Boring, blaming, belittling,
Unkind, uncaring, unfaithful.

You steal away again.
I read my novel,
Keep company with the dog,
Nurture my own patience.
I've almost saved enough
To toss you.
Then she will own
The flip side.

Maui Miracle

Lynne C. Gregg

"Look, the islands!" Mark spied several small black spots in the huge Pacific. When the plane swooped in an arc, it was then they could see the beauty of the turquoise water, crashing waves and cliffs of Maui.

The excitement built as they made the final approach for landing. Lynne could see the all the colorful flowers from the air in every direction she looked. "Angels must have planted those flowers for thousands of years to create such a paradise after the volcanoes did their job."

It was a vacation they had dreamed of for years, but this year it was special in a sentimental way. They planned to honor the memory of their daughter Angela who had become an angel one year ago on Valentine's Day. After landing, Mark and Lynne were greeted by smiling Hawaiian natives with an "Aloha" and leis to place around their necks.

Lynne adjusted her lei and her voice cracked a little as she fought to hold back tears, "We're here in memory of our girl. I can't believe we'll experience all the wonders as she once she did—especially seeing the whales."

Mark was tall, fifty-ish, and loved travel. He was also a guy who never got lost while driving on their many trips. Lynne appreciated this because she had no sense of direction. He never worried about anything back home when they traveled. "Life is too short not to see the world – especially in a Mustang convertible!" He bought sensible cars for his personal use, but he always splurged on vacation rental cars. He wasn't as excited as Lynne to see the whales, but he loved her excitement.

Lynne also loved to travel. She wanted to see as much of the world as she could. She had a funny sense of humor and always upbeat; her cup was not half full or half empty, but rather, it was always overflowing. She tended to become excited about each new thing she experienced, but that made her all the more endearing to her husband. "You know, Lynne, you're a lot of fun to travel with, and you're pretty cute, too."

"Why thank you, sir, but keep your hand off my leg and on that stick shift. I have my reputation to think of."

Lynne had done her homework. Their February vacation timing was exactly right. She knew the whales made the three thousand mile swim from Alaska and wintered in Baja and Maui where the brochures said they *calved* or had their babies. The whales were bottom swimmers in the warm waters surrounding the Hawaiian Islands, and the sand on the ocean floor rubbed off all the barnacles that attached in the cold waters near Alaska. "I want to see their slick black and white enormous bodies."

They arrived at their hotel and were delighted to have a third floor balcony room overlooking the ocean. Lynne immediately scanned the water with her binoculars, "I just spotted a whale breeching far off-shore. Come and look, Mark! Maybe there are more."

Mark couldn't hide the excitement in his voice. "Yep! I see 'em, too!"

"When do we sign up for our whale boat trip out to the reefs where they feed? I want to see then up close and personal!"

"I'll walk down to the hotel desk and ask about the trips now. What day do you want to go?"

"Any day but Valentine's Day. That day is reserved for us and our angel."

Besides sight-seeing and whale-watching, Lynne and Mark had more reasons for this trip. They had both just retired. They would be on Maui for Valentine's Day. "Could there be a more romantic place for us to celebrate the day of love?" Lynne winked at Mark as they drove along a windy highway with the top down on their black Mustang.

Sadly, February 14th also marked the first anniversary of their daughter, Angela's death. Lynne knew Angela was an angel and that she dropped pennies from heaven to her from time to time to say, "I love you, Mom." Mark just smiled at her with a skeptical look on his face when she picked them up with a "Thank you, Sweetie. I love you, too."

Angela had worked in Hawaii in management with an airline as her first job after graduating from the University of Texas. Lynne's favorite pictures of Angela were the ones she sent from Maui. Instead of being sad on this first anniversary of losing her older daughter, Lynne planned to choose a beautiful lei in memory of Angela, wear it all day on Valentine's Day, and then at sunset, throw the lei into the ocean. Lynne knew she would feel Angela's spirit touch her face on the ocean breezes. She believed her girl was an angel. "Look at her name!"

Along with the whale watching boat trip that proved more wonderful than Lynne had ever imagined, they went to a pineapple plantation and viewed the entire process from plants to canned fruit ready to be shipped off the island. They also went to a sugar cane museum. They both loved this kind of sightseeing never hurrying one another as they learned new things.

During this stay on Maui, Lynne and Mark, for the first time, flew in a helicopter. They went up 10,000 feet to the top of a volcano. Then they flew over the rim where they saw the splendor of over one hundred waterfalls cascading down the sides of the inactive volcano. As they sped up and out again, they saw rainbows in every direction. The chopper was noisy. They could only point at breath-taking sights as they listened to the music in their headsets. During their flight they flew very close to the surface of the ocean. To Lynne's joy, they saw a pod of breeching whales—blowholes spewing, mamas with calves, and tails slapping the ocean surface before the whales dove below.

Before they knew it, Valentine's Day had arrived. They went to a lei market, and Lynne spotted the lei she wanted almost instantly. It was very unusual, with alternating red carnations and purple orchids. Mark placed it over her head, adjusted it on her shoulders, and kissed his wife gently on the cheek. "You look beautiful. I'm glad we made this trip so we could be here today."

It was a beautiful lei. It was nothing like Lynne had imagined she'd buy, but she wore it all day filled with memories of Angela. "It makes me feel so close to my Ang. It still seems impossible she's been gone a year." Angela's death came without warning when she finally wore out from a lifetime of battling juvenile diabetes. She was only thirty-four.

Mark wrapped his arm around Lynne's shoulder and agreed. "Whenever I think of her, I can still hear her laughter. I pray I never forget the sound. Even though her life was difficult, especially the last year and half after she lost her sight, she never lost her sense of humor."

They had selected a restaurant from their piles of brochures, and Mark made reservations for an early dinner. "We need to make sure we have time to get to the pier by sunset."

At the restaurant Lynne noticed a couple about their age sitting at the next table with a young woman. Lynne guessed she might be their grown daughter, possibly visiting them on Maui. Every time Lynne looked up, the older woman was staring at her. Lynne mentioned this to Mark who seemed unconcerned. "She probably likes your lei."

Finally the woman spoke, "I love your lei."

"Thank you. I love it, too." Lynne lightly touched one of the red carnations.

Mark had a smug look on his face but refrained from saying, "I told you so."

They made a few other bits of polite conversation with the woman about the whales and the weather, and then the waiter brought a long-stemmed red rose on the tray with their wonderful seafood dinners.

Once Lynne looked up while she was eating, and the older woman was asking her daughter if she had any angels in her purse. Lynne thought that was a little weird, but, hey, she was eavesdropping on their conversation! Throughout the meal, Lynne noticed the woman watching her. They made eye contact several times and smiled.

When they were finished eating, Mark stayed to sign the credit card bill, and Lynne headed for the ladies' room. As she walked by the other couple's table, the woman stopped her to admire the lei and asked if it was a Valentine's gift. Lynne said, "Sort of. I am wearing this in memory of our daughter who passed away a year ago today. We ate dinner early so we could go out on a pier and toss the lei to her in the ocean at sunset."

The woman's face turned compassionate and she said, "I'm so sorry that you had to come to Maui for such a sad occasion.

"Oh, no," Lynne said. "We're here to celebrate our retirements. It just happened that we planned the trip months ago, and it fell on the anniversary of her death. She worked on Oahu after college, and I have wonderful memories and pictures of her hops to Maui with friends, so this seemed like a perfect way to remember her. In fact my life is filled with joy. My other daughter is expecting triplets!"

"You're kidding! Triplets. How wonderful!" She wished them a pleasant stay as Lynne left to look for the restrooms.

When Lynne walked out of the bathroom stall, the woman was standing there. She said, "I just had to follow you. Hold out your hand." Then she sprinkled those little confetti angels into Lynne's open palm.

Lynne smiled. "Why thank you. My daughter's name was Angela, and many people gave us gifts of angels, but these are my first confetti angels."

"So that's it. I felt a connection with you as soon as we sat down. I kept seeing the word angel every time I made eye contact with you," she said. "May I ask you a couple of questions? Feel free to not answer me or just walk away if you like."

Lynne felt safe and rather hooked on what the question might be, so she told her, "Ask away."

"First of all, who are Kendra and Kelly? Those names would not go away once I saw you."

Calmly Lynne told her this story: "My daughter Liz, the one who is expecting triplets, went to high school and college with a girl named Kendra. Kendra had a twin, but Liz and Kendra looked more like twins than Kendra and her twin sister. In fact, Kendra's mom and I often took pictures of each other's daughters by mistake. Liz recently went to a Mothers of Multiples web page on her computer and signed in as *Liz O from The Woodlands*. Someone immediately replied, 'Oh, you must be Kendra's friend.'"

"Liz told the person she must be mistaken because she only knew one Kendra and they have been out of Texas A & M for twelve years and have had no contact.

"But the person on-line described them looking like twins, their moms taking the wrong pictures, etc., so Liz told her that Kendra must be her old friend from high school and college.

"Next, the on-line person told Liz that Kendra had just had triplets, two boys and a girl—exactly what Liz was expecting."

Lynne had been amazed by the coincidence that Liz and Kendra both were going to be mothers of triplets, but how did this unknown woman in Hawaii know the name Kendra? It isn't exactly a common name. And the woman nodded her head the entire time Lynne told the story as if she already knew it.

The woman said, "I have one more question if you will put up with me."

Lynne figured, "What the heck? This has proven to be rather interesting so far."

"Who is Kelly?" she asked.

"Angela and Kelly were very close friends in high school. One week after graduation, Angela was driving, they had a terrible car accident, and Kelly was killed. Angela never got over it."

The woman said, "I could not get the name Kelly out of my head. I knew she was somehow related to an angel. Well, let me tell you this: Angela and Kelly are together as angels, and they are looking down smiling on you right now."

Lynne was speechless, but an odd sense of warmth encompassed her body.

Next the woman said, "Angela was married, wasn't she, but just a short time?"

Lynne couldn't believe her ears, "Oh, yes, to Paul, a big red-head, her teddy bear. They were only married a year and three months, but he made her life complete. I'll never quit loving him for that."

The woman held out her hand in introduction and said, "Hi, I'm Paula."

"I'm Lynne." She felt great—especially about Angela and Kelly together in heaven.

Paula handed Lynne a card that read, "Upper Peninsula Miracles." This woman practiced ESP on a Christian level. Lynne asked her, "How do you deal with all the skeptics?"

"In response to that I guess I'd say when someone is willing, he or she can remember the truth as a spirit—or a connection to one's higher self. Sort of like during the Sixties being 'tuned in, tapped in, and turned on to the spirit. I enjoy it all. Email me if you ever have any more questions or thoughts. I'd love to hear from you."

Lynne had to explain why she was in the restroom for fifteen minutes with a perfect stranger when she walked out to find a pacing Mark. "I thought I was going to have to come in and rescue you."

Lynne handed Mark part of her handful of angels. Mark and Lynne both held them as Lynne tossed her lei into the Pacific. At the hotel they put them away in two different places in their luggage in hotel envelopes. In case they lost some, they would still have some as keepsakes.

The rest of the trip was pleasant. Occasionally, Lynne would catch herself thinking about Paula and the angels.

Amazingly, the angels have all flown away to join Angela and Kelly in heaven because Lynne and Mark can find them nowhere. Lynne emailed Paula to tell her the angels had mysteriously flown away. She also told her that Angela had been the practical joker in the family. "She's probably chuckling every time I looked for those angels."

"Oh, she knows where those angels are. Without a doubt in my mind," Paula typed back.

This is a true story. Lynne's daughter, Angela, died way too young. Both mother and daughter were avid readers, story tellers, and great friends. Paula from *Upper Peninsula Miracles* is a Christian woman who practices E.S.P.

Too Good to Be False

Guida Jackson

One day in the spring of 1974 my friend Julia Gomez-Rivas called to say she had just seen an ad in the Greensheet for a writers class to be conducted by Phyllis Stillwell Prokop. Since neither of us had heard of this teacher, Julia decided to call for more information. She spoke to someone named Jane Chenevert who said the classes would be held in her home, near us in Houston's Memorial area. We still didn't know anything about Phyllis, but the price was right, and the daytime hour suited us, since our children would be in school at that time. Julia signed on for both of us.

Phyllis, it turned out, had a long resume, but she was modest to a fault, and it took us several weeks to learn much about her. She had a master's degree in English and was the author of several books published by Broadman, David C. Cook, and others. Above all, from our standpoint, she was an excellent teacher. The good teachers I have known throughout life have been long on encouragement and short on criticism. That was Phyllis.

Phyllis and her sister were born and raised on a farm near Weleetka, Oklahoma, by strict, pious Baptist parents. She remained true to her upbringing for her entire life. During the early days of World War II, she married Naval recruit Charles Prokop, recent graduate of the University of Oklahoma with a degree in Petroleum Engineering.

They had a limited amount of money and very little time to be together before Charles was to ship out of New Orleans. Phyllis followed Charles to New Orleans and was staying in a hotel near the docks. Charles explained that he wouldn't be able to get word to her if the ship had sailed, but until it received orders to depart, he could come to her every day, and they would spend a frugal honeymoon together. Each morning Phyllis waited anxiously for him to appear, and each day for over a week, he did.

But they soon had a new worry. Their money was almost gone. Phyllis was going to have to check out of the hotel the next day and go back to Oklahoma, even before Charles shipped out. As they walked down the street toward her hotel that last day, they looked down at their feet and saw a wad of bills lying on the sidewalk! There was no way to know who the owner was, in that town full of transients. They took the money and considered it a gift from God that enabled them to spend a few more days together. After all, who knew if Charles would ever come back?

On the last day, when the new money had also run out and Phyllis was preparing to tell Charles she must leave that day, he did not appear. His ship had sailed during the night. Phyllis could not tell this story thirty years later without crying at the wonder of it.

While Charles was in the Navy, he once found himself with a couple of other sailors in a very small boat floating in the Aleutians. One man asked Charles where he was from, and when he learned Charles was from Oklahoma, the man said, "You wouldn't happen to know Phyllis Jean Stillwell from Weleetka, would you?" Even then, Phyllis had a magnetic personality that was hard to forget. Charles certainly never forgot what a marvel he had, and his devotion was evident. Whenever Phyllis had an autograph party, or was to be guest speaker at a function, Charles took off work to attend. When our group spent several days at the beach, Charles would appear to be sure we had everything we needed.

If I were asked to summarize my description of Phyllis in one word, it would be 'Christian'. She was first and foremost a fundamentalist Christian, not the kind of person I would usually seek out. But Phyllis was a very wise one who evinced her beliefs with actions and not words. Among our group— who became her best friends—was a life-long Zen Buddhist, a couple of flower children, a New Ager, three Catholics, a feminist, a hard-drinking alcoholic, and a Jungian. Phyllis treated all with the same non-judgmental respect.

She was genuinely interested in our views. At each meeting she would introduce a topic she'd been thinking about and researching, and we would voice our own opinions while Phyllis took notes. We learned so much from those sessions, from Phyllis and from each other. She knew how to draw out the best in us.

Above everything else, she was an optimist, probably because of her rock-hard faith. We felt good being in her presence. Her disposition was contagious, and through more than a quarter of a century—actually, thirty-nine years—the members of that class have adopted that same optimistic attitude. Over the years we have laughed much more often than we have cried.

Our class consisted of students who would become life-long friends, have frequent parties that were most often autograph parties for one or the other of us, and who would convene at least once yearly for a several-day retreat at

Galveston: Ida Luttrell, Gloria Wahlen, Jane Chenevert, Olivia Orfield, Lynda Jackson, Carol Rowe Bennett (DeBender), Julia Gomez-Rivas, Sharon Boswell, and Susan Fifer. Later we would add Mary Schomaker, Nell Harris, Doris Bird, Donna Wolfe, Pat Kochera, Joyce Pounds Hardy, and Frances Chapman (McMaster). Six, including Phyllis, have died. Four have moved away. The rest of us still meet and still quote Phyllis frequently.

Charles had a stellar career with Exxon that had eventually landed them in Houston, where they bought an Art-Deco house in the area behind the Shamrock, in which they entertained often. Phyllis loved to cook and sometimes invited us to lunch. Once during our sessions, she got the idea to put together a cookbook consisting of recipes with only three ingredients, for busy people like us. We were invited to participate in this project, and when it was time to assemble the manuscript, she talked a doctor she knew who had a vacant, fully furnished Victorian mansion on Broadway in Galveston into allowing us to use it for several days. She badgered her Broadman editor into taking the book, and she shared the royalties with us all.

She and Charles had two sons, Kent and Kendall, who both married and moved away, one to Tulsa. When Charles retired, they decided to move to Tulsa to be nearer to family. Charles bought Phyllis a large house and immersed himself in affairs of the community, as did Phyllis. Later, when Kent left Tulsa, Charles asked Phyllis what she wanted to do next. She said, "I want to go home." Whatever Phyllis wanted is what he gave her. They returned to Weleetka, where her sister still lived. They didn't move to the farm but got a very nice house in town.

It was there that Charles learned he had cancer. Phyllis, who handled everything else under the sun with aplomb, became frantic to save him. She must have spent many hours on her knees, wrestling with the Lord, cajoling Him to spare the most wonderful man—besides her father—she had ever known. But the Lord who had provided so bounteously throughout her life would not spare Charles this injustice, even for her. After a long, painful, and valiant struggle, he died, never having to know that the love of his life had by then developed Alzheimer's. We often wondered how Phyllis would ever get along without Charles. As it happened, she was spared years of bereft desolation by her own disease.

Soon the boys had to place Phyllis, who remained at least outwardly her old sunny self, in a special facility, where she died peacefully a year or so later. Those of us whom she had shepherded and mentored would never forget her love and support; would quote her often; would laugh again at her frequently told stories. I see that radiant face in my mind's eye and mentally say, "Phyllis, if ever there was a child of God, you are a special one. And if ever there was a heaven, you earned a place in it."

Guida Jackson-Laufer is the author of more than a dozen books on women in history and women's issues. She lives in the Houston area and is revered as a mentor to many writers.

Buckle Up For Love

Melanie Ormand

The rhythmic forward motion of the rental car slowed then stopped. I opened my eyes and blinked. Hard. A flood of late June sun gushed over me through the right rear window. An hour earlier I had sprawled out across the back seat for a post-lunch nap while a comforting blanket of yellow-white rays had warmed me to sleep. But as the car rolled to a stop I groaned and turned my face into my makeshift pillow, a scrunched-up wad of rain jacket, fleece hoodie, and my canvas backpack.

The car idled, engine purring, air conditioner humming. I could see the back of my husband's head as he sat behind the steering wheel without speaking. It was the first day of our long-planned road trip from Colorado north to Montana.

Where in hell are we? I wondered.

Suddenly the front passenger window slid down and a wave of hot summer air burst into the car. My husband's voice—strong, confident and smooth as honey, a tribute to his three decades as a radio broadcaster—rolled across the front seat.

"Hello, Officer," he said, "how are you today?"

I rolled my eyes. *Here we go,* I thought, *Chuck. Speeding. Again. Welcome to our vacation.* Groping around the backseat for my sunglasses, I realized I had no idea where we were. I scanned the horizon. A monotonous landscape surrounded us, filled with acres of hills topped with dead yellow grass, an assortment of black, brown, and white cows, and an occasional oil rig identifiable by its blue steel frame.

A figure clothed in olive green filled the passenger window.

"Honey, he's talking to you," I heard Chuck's voice—louder than usual—now speaking directly to me. I looked up to see his brown eyes gazing directly at mine. He cocked his head toward the open window. My heart leaped into my throat. I fumbled for my hearing aids, both tucked earlier into the pockets behind the front seat. Hands shaking, I jammed them into my ears.

"Ma'am?" a strange voice directed itself at me.

"Yes?" my earlier mind fog vanished in a nanosecond.

"Your license, please," his no-nonsense voice felt uncomfortably familiar. I looked at Chuck. He shrugged and said nothing. My ears began to pound in confusion.

My license? What the hell was this? *What could I have possibly done wrong? I was sleeping!* I dug in my backpack and handed him my license.

"Ma'am, I noticed that you did not have your seatbelt on," the trooper's voice droned. "In the state of Wyoming, everyone in the car must be buckled up when the car is in motion."

I had a sudden and overwhelming urge to burst out in multiple, multi-syllabic profanities. *You've got to be kidding me,* I thought.

"Even when you're in the back seat? Asleep?"

"If you'd seen what I've seen," he said ominously, "you'd always buckle up."

"But I'm from Texas," the words stuttered out of me. I could not believe what I was hearing. My lungs tightened. I took a deep breath. My heart thumped hard in my chest. I struggled to stay rational. I opened my eyes wide, hoping to feminize the conversation. I knew I was about to get a ticket, and I figured I should use what I had.

"What I'm saying, Officer," I said sweetly, "is I'm not familiar with the laws in Wyoming."

That's so lame. I thought, *you can do better than that.*

The trooper smiled at me as I spoke. His teeth gleamed. Mirrored sunglasses hid his eyes. The deep olive of his uniform—hat, shirt, pants, and belt— reminded me more of the Canadian Mounted police and less of an American law enforcement officer. For a second, my mind wondered if this man wasn't fake and we were about to find out that we had been punked.

"I fully understand," his deep bass voice spoke with a confidence that fit the power he owned right then. "But it is the law in Wyoming. Everyone, sleeping or awake, front seat or back, must be buckled up. No exceptions."

I glanced at Chuck, the person who, after all, was the driver who had been caught speeding, who had landed me in this mess of the moment. As I looked at my husband, memories flew by of him holding other pink citations—all for speeding, of course—and weekend plans busted by yet another last-minute defensive driving course. Violent marital thoughts—of the type that could land me inside state prison—raced through my mind. Chuck shrugged.

Thanks for the help, Honey.

"Yes, sir, Trooper," I smiled back. "I understand."

The trooper handed me the pink citation for my signature. When I finished, he tipped his hat then turned to Chuck.

"And your license, sir?" he extended his right hand through the front passenger window.

The police radio on his hip squawked with the voice of a female dispatcher. He twisted the volume knob and the radio went silent. "You are aware that you were speeding—74 miles per hour in a 65 mile-per-hour zone?"

With a tenderness that belied his six-foot-plus frame, Chuck placed his license in the trooper's palm. He removed his sunglasses and leaned across the passenger seat.

"I thought the speed limit was 75 or maybe 80 out here on the open range." With his left hand, he waved at the landscape that surrounded us. His eyes never left the trooper. "The sign read 75 miles per hour back there at the state line so I figured that the speed limit was that or more for the rest of Wyoming."

"I'm sorry, sir, that's not the case," the trooper said, "but it's the July 4th holiday weekend. So I'll let you off with a warning and give your wife the ticket. Hers is only $10 but for speeding yours would be $85 or more, depending on the judge. I'll save you both a little money this way."

Chuck smiled. Broadly. My blood began to simmer then boil in my veins.

"Thanks for the break, Officer," he said.

"Slow it down and buckle up, will you?" With that, the trooper winked at both of us, turned and walked back to his cruiser.

I caught Chuck's brown eyes, gazing large and wet—and filled with child-like innocence—at me through the rear view mirror.

"Gosh, I'm sorry, honey," he started, "I get stopped for speeding and you get the ticket."

In spite of myself, I laughed. The absurdity of the moment marked a simultaneous high and low moment—a first in our twenty-seven adventurous years together.

"We're changing places," I gave my husband no options, "Now."

Scrambling like a monkey, I scooted from the back seat to the front and landed with a dull 'plop' on the hot vinyl. "I'm driving now."

Moments later, I sat with a fiery and firm confidence in the driver's seat, my fingers drumming an urgent beat on the steering wheel. With exaggerated—and loud—motion, I buckled the seatbelt, pulling it tight across my waist.

Cackling with devilish glee, I winked at Chuck. He lay half-sprawled against the back seat, readying himself for a nap. When he heard my foot gun the engine, his eyes widened as my fingers tightened on the pink citation still clutched in my left hand. "Here we go, sweetheart, better buckle up!"

After working 20 years as both an award-winning journalist and a crisis communications consultant, Melanie Ormand now writes full-time.

Her current projects include a non-fiction, self-help book for people experiencing sudden health crises—like the ruptured brain aneurysm she herself suffered last year. Fiction works in progress include a novel and a suspense/adventure quadrilogy for women. Melanie also routinely pens short stories and poetry to vary both her form and creative practice.

Melanie has been published/broadcast in *The Sun* magazine, NPR's "This I Believe" program and numerous anthologies. She blogs regularly on her website, www.melanieormand.com and tweets when she feels like it. During her earlier careers in print, broadcast news and communications consulting, Melanie frequently published articles and spoke to trade groups.

Thankful for the Tragedy

Monica Stanton

Today Barbara would have been married to her husband for fifty years. She told me as we were leaving church. Barbara is a widow and my first thought was to comfort her, except she was so darn happy! "If I were still married to that man, I would be dead!" Barbara chimed. The ecstatic widow smiled and literally bounced into her shiny, white SUV.

I met Barbara a week ago, along with fifteen other remarkable women, at my first women's Bible study. So what does a group of Bible thumping women have to do with love in today's world? Everything. I was amazed to learn a majority of these women had many problems just like me, including a few that were recently divorced. After twenty years of marriage, I was three months into being single and struggling with the stigma of being divorced and being alone. It is not easy starting over at the age of fifty-two, though it was my choice and I was ready to figure out this new life.

I have learned my divorce story is eerily repeated by women I thought never would have such dire issues sneak into their Christian lives. For years, in silence and from the distance of causal glances across the church aisle I admired these women for their beautiful grace and sweet families. I dreamed of their evenings, laughing as they enjoyed dinner around the dining room table, children sharing stories of educational success or another sports victory. I saw these women as knowing scriptures by heart to encourage every need. I could see each one smile as her husband's lips gingerly kissed her forehead as he thanked her for another perfect dinner. I never dreamed these women would have issues, let alone tragedies.

I accidentally found out about my ex-husband's vast money problems while attempting to refinance our home. Adding scary, hidden, financial data to other, not very nice stuff I had learned to live with through twenty years, it was time to move on. Yet I felt so alone and tiny. I never shared my problems, fearful of what might happen to me if my husband found out. I had been all alone for years and now, I found the sisterhood that had always been there.

Much heartbreak was shared that first night at Bible study together. One lost a brother. Another had a struggling teenager. Several were recently divorced as I was. One had just found a job after being unemployed for five months. One had a toddler daughter with a rare ailment – my heart ached as a mother described the pain and the tubes and the medical tests. Our children are not meant to suffer so. An amazing discussion of how to not run from your live but to live through it. The lesson was to practice thankfulness in every instance. My heart opened as if I were learning of grace for the very first time. Possibly this was the first time I understood it.

I am thankful for my children. I could focus on them and be so grateful forever. Last week, I came home from work exhausted. I opened the door to the forceful scent of matches, too many burnt candles and scorched hair. Panic swelled from my stomach, taking my breath, my eyes tearing and then in an instant the panic was gone as I discovered my fifteen year-old son in the kitchen with a blow dryer and matches. He had painted a three foot by five foot piece of plywood white. Across the top of the board he had glued crayons, sixty-four of them, the entire Crayola box, all side-by-side, the paper still intact. He melted each waxy crayon into the next. The yellows blended with the blues and greens layered over the reds, long drip lines of color on fresh bright white. The wax was still hot and shiny, creating ambers of brilliant colors. There were amazing tiny bubbles of brightness just holding on to the end of each long, soft line. "Mom, I saw the idea on the computer and thought it was cool," my son broadly smiled. Children are amazing. A masterpiece was created.

I love to work on my computer, comfy in my soft leather recliner tucked in the corner of the living room. Weeks after the divorce, a group of teens were baking cookies, cooking dinner, laughing, teasing. And they were all totally ignoring me. Just being good kids hanging out on a Friday night. My seventeen year old son was even cleaning in the kitchen! Peace had come back to our home. It was so nice and calm and joyful. Most of the jokes I did not understand. Some of the boys used words I would have preferred they did not use. Yet they were all safe and having fun. A gathering of youth would not have happened if I were still married.

My sons and I are remodeling the home I was able to keep. Homes are important. We are tearing out carpet, painting rooms, and laying tile all on our own. Demolishing the old and bringing in the new. I have to agree with every person who has ever said how much they appreciate his or her own labor. It would look the same (or maybe even better) if we hired it out, but today we grew closer together because we loved our home one tile at a time.

I know in a few years my sons will move on to start their own lives in their own homes. I need to consider what I am to do if I am to truly become a new person after divorce. I was beginning to understand the need to see myself as someone too.

It all happened one morning. To wake up in a home where you feel safe and comfortable after years of fear is amazing. It must be the feeling a person gets when they win the lottery. The tingling, slow motion seconds of realization that the rest of your life will be different. I stretched out my arms, the blankets fell away and the first morning light was only enough to make shadows of branches on the walls. I then realized I was truly safe and calm. Thankfulness. It was a really good day.

I will never be sure if I had the right kind of love to keep my marriage together forever. Or even if keeping my marriage together would have been the right thing to do. Maybe, like Barbara, my marriage truly was killing me a little at a time. Today's loss is a new beginning. We do not live in an easy world. Horrible tragedies can be found in an instant. So can the good in people. Look into the world and be thankful.

But could I be thankful for the ugly in my life? For years I pulled into myself, a tight cocoon of fear and shame. No one knew the true me, how I felt lost, bankrupt and invisible. I accomplished little and did not understand how I had let my life become so filled with fear and shame. Could I be thankful? What about my ailing parents and a strained relationship through years of hiding myself from them? I had not visited them in years. I missed my parents and was grateful they were still alive.

I had an idea for a fantastic project related to victims of drunk drivers and had struggled to make progress for the last three years. At times I have not been sure I had the strength or the aptitude. Now I am driven to make the project work. To honor those who have been through so much more that I will ever know. I see the good as I see it will offer hope and help the blameless. There were times I doubted myself because I was told I was not worthy. Never again will I doubt my ability or my fortitude as I want these families of tragedy to know that they are not alone nor are they forgotten.

My ex-husband told me I was weak, worthless, ugly, and stupid. I let him make me feel worthless. He threatened many bad things if I left him. Some bad things did happen. He threatened never to spend time with our two beautiful sons. He definitely achieved hurting me financially. The day we divorced I had

$300 to my name and a mountain of debt. I will be fine. I have a dependable job, and I am more courageous every day.

Starting over is just that. I feel twenty-five. I feel free, and I do not see the wrinkles when I look in the mirror. I see the pretty green eyes smiling back. Like Barbara, I have greatly increased my life expectancy.

What I learned through the first meeting of my new-found friends is you do not have to go through life alone. These women are amazing, just as I had always envisioned. Not because they had perfect lives, but because they knew they were in the perfect place for the life they are living. Thankfulness is the first step towards a life filled with love. It is not easy to be thankful for a messed up life that needed a restart, though I am thankful my restart began by meeting Barbara.

Monica Stanton is a single mother of two teenage boys. She spends time with her family, learning, writing, working and reading. She graduated from college in Corning, NY and works full time in the oil and gas industry.

Her current project, *White Crosses of Houston,* is a collection of stories of the impact of drunk driving. Monica has been interviewing families whose loved ones have been killed or critically injured by drunk drivers. Proceeds from the sale of her books will go into White Crosses of America, a non-profit agency dedicated to providing scholarships to children who have lost their parents to drunk drivers.

Moving On

Janet Nash

The electronic door swished open as Lisa England entered the brand new superstore. She nodded to the cordial elderly greeter and snagged a shopping cart. Slipping her cargo purse off of her shoulder, she tossed it into her basket. *Now where is my list?* After patting her pockets and coming up empty, she tangled with her purse. First pouch, nada, second pouch, nothing. Rustling through the center compartment of her bag, she lifted a handful of dog-eared papers. She stopped dead in her tracks as if she had run into a brick wall. The note buried in her hand shook her to the core.

The handwriting was his. The familiar backward slant of each letter reminded her of the funny way he wrote left handed. The date in the top left corner caught her eye – 11/11. Nearly a year had passed, a turbulent year. Yet she hadn't stumbled across the note until now. She melted into a daze.

"Excuse me." A gentle voice interrupted her stupor. Blinking away her thoughts, Lisa shifted her gaze and stared at the gentleman behind the voice. He was tall, a tad unshaven and had warm milk-chocolate eyes. Softened by his striking good looks, she bit back the 'you're a sight for sore eyes' that almost escaped her mouth. Her lips twitched into a small smile.

"Aren't you ..." He snapped his fingers. "Lisa um ..., the lady from ..."

"Yes I am." Disappointment sagged her shoulders and weariness softened her voice. When would it stop? She plucked her sunglasses from her purse and tried to hide behind them.

"I'm sorry. I didn't mean to upset you. I ..." His glance darted to the ground.

"Is there something you need?" A silence as thick as putty hung in the air. He never responded, seemingly embarrassed by her curtness. After a few awkward seconds, Lisa just wheeled away. What else could she do? She hated feeling like she was *on display*.

"Wait, you ..." Too uncomfortable to turn around, she blazed ahead swerving her cart through scores of shoppers. After a sharp left, she landed in the condiment isle. She glanced back to be sure he hadn't followed. She puffed out a sigh and leaned on her basket.

There were disadvantages to living in a small town like Ludowici, Georgia. Everyone knew everything about everybody, and Lisa had her day in the spot light. Not as a celebrity or a hometown hero. As a headline, the kind of newsflash that people would talk about for years.

The scandal was over eleven months ago. She already collected on the life insurance for Max and donated all of his clothes to Goodwill. The ring finger on her left hand no longer had the indented groove from her wedding band. And she was more determined than ever to keep moving on.

"Excuse me," a woman's voice whispered. Lisa jumped, startled out of her pity party. "I'm sorry, I need a bottle of Heinz 57." The woman pointed to the row of sauces just behind Lisa's head. She scooted her basket out of the way, turned back and grinned at the polite shopper. At this point, Lisa couldn't even remember why she was in the store. She tucked the note back into her purse, impulsively lifted her bag from the cart and rushed out to the parking lot.

Sitting in her car, she gripped the steering wheel, nearly pulling it from the dash and stared at the bumper sticker of the Toyota parked in front of her: Have a nice day. A torrent of emotions stirred up many flavors of anxiety and memories of that day. That dreadful day. Her husband, a financial planner, swindled dozens of retired locals out of their life's savings. A Ponzi scam gone bad. He never made it to trial. He chose the easy way out, suicide. Each and every day since his death, Lisa woke up and tried to start life anew. Finding out she'd been married to a liar and a cheat for ten years, then his leaving her alone to pick up all of the pieces had taken its toll. Maybe she should just pack up and leave this town?

"Tap, tap, tap." Lisa turned and her breath caught in her throat. It was him.

"I'm sorry to bother you, can you roll down..." His muffled voice was kind, yet his breathing seemed labored. The muscles in his jaw pulsated as he signaled for her to lower her window. She opened the window, enough to hear, and raised her brow.

"I just wanted to apologize and . . . Please don't think ..."

"No need to apologize. I'm fine. If you don't mind, I'm in a hurry." She gazed into his dark autumn eyes and felt her heart beat quicken. On impulse, she rolled up her window. Out of the corner of her eye, she saw him holding out his hand as he stepped back from her car. As fast as she could, she started the engine, shifted into reverse, and high-tailed it out of there.

Lisa landed at home not sure what had happened. Who was that guy anyway? You don't just go up and talk to strangers. Assured she did nothing wrong by ignoring his unsolicited conversation, she buried herself in work. There were at least sixty papers to grade, and they were all due tomorrow. She also needed to prepare for Meet the Parents night. Telling strangers that their third grader possessed a kindergarten reading level wasn't something she looked forward to doing. But there was an upside. Several of her new spry eight year olds showed promise of being shining stars. She couldn't wait to brag to their parents. Her thoughts swirled back to the gentleman at the store. *I hope none of the parents recognize me.*

The day started out like any other. Two cups of coffee, loads of traffic, and a broken finger nail. Lisa breezed through the day reading to her third grade class. The joyful first week of school gets the kids hooked, kind of reading readiness. Though she always seemed hurried, she managed to maintain a smile. She loved teaching reading. It defined her.

Not long after the final bell, she prepared the classroom for Meet the Parents night. Her bright colorful collage spotlighting C. S. Lewis was ready for viewing.

The teachers' lounge sported a spread of six inch sub sandwiches, baked chips and iced tea. Fed and relaxed, Lisa hustled to her classroom and reviewed her appointment schedule. The first batch of eager parents started rolling in. Lisa did the usual meet and greet, then pointed the moms and dads to her Wall of Fame. She posted each student's top essays for easy viewing. About an hour later, the informal school affair was coming to a close. While handing out graded papers, Lisa eyed a man walking through the door. Her gut wrenched in surprise. It was him. *How could it be? Is he following me?* He stopped. With his eyes like saucers, his rugged jaw dropped. It was obvious he wasn't expecting to see her.

Lisa focused on slow and measured breaths and reminded herself that she had nothing to be afraid of. She harnessed her anxiety, shook a few hands, and walked toward him. Now face to face, Lisa ruffled her feathers and stood strong. "Hi, I'm Lisa England." She reached out her hand.

The warmth of his grip calmed her nerves.

"Well hello, Lisa England. It's a pleasure to actually meet you." He grinned.

"Can I ask why you're here?"

"This is room 33, right?"

"Yes."

"My son, Ethan, is in this class. Ethan Kelly. I'm Josh." He released her hand.

She concentrated on hiding the flush that had crept into her face. "Why did you stop me in the store?"

"Hold on." Josh slid the wallet from his back pocket and plucked out a piece of paper. "You dropped this." He handed her a small folded piece of paper.

"That's why you stopped me? Because I dropped this." Her eyes widened and her knickers fluttered. "But you said my name."

"As soon as you turned around I recognized you from the news last year. I didn't know what else to say."

Lisa unfolded the note in her hand. It didn't take long to read the hand written two sentences scribbled on the page. 'A great website to meet a man. Matchmaker.com.' She remembered her friend Gail tucking the note in her purse a few weeks back. Hopefully, that was the only paper that fell from the pile she held in the store. She also recalled the conversation they had. It was time to move on and Lisa knew it, she just didn't know where to begin. An overwhelming sensation of hope washed over her as she looked up at Josh.

"Mind it I ask what it says?" Josh raised his brow.

"You mean you had this note in your wallet and you never read it?"

"It was folded, I didn't want to… I was curious. I am curious." Josh grinned.

Goose bumps tickled Lisa. She took in a deep breath, "I can't believe you didn't look. What were you planning to do with it?"

He twitched his brows and tightened his lips, "I don't know. I guess I was hoping to run into you again."

"You didn't know I was Ethan's teacher, did you?"

"No, I didn't. It sure was a nice surprise." Josh smiled brightly.

Lisa shook hands with the last group of parents leaving her meet and greet. A grand overall joy caused her to giggle as she returned her focus to Josh. He grinned with softened eyes. She moseyed to her Wall of Fame and pointed out Ethan's paper. She blushed and asked, "You know you're late, don't you?"

"I know. It's a bad habit. Forgive me?"

She smiled with her eyes. "Aren't you still curious about the note?"

Josh blinked slow and deliberate. "Not really. I'd love a cup of coffee. You want to join me?"

Lisa tucked the paper into her pocket. "I'd love to."

Janet Nash, born and raised in Chicago, is an RWA 2012 Golden Heart Finalist. She moved to Texas 30 years ago and never looked back. In 2005 writing took over her life when she was inspired to write a story. The past seven years she absorbing everything she could to master the craft of writing. The journey has far exceeded her expectations and has grown into passion. Her first book has now been published.

Jared's Song

Jaye Garland

Ten thirty in the morning and her name was still Shelby Rae Turner. By now, it should have been Shelby Rae Hanson. Where the hell was he? Why didn't he show up?

She fingered the lace veil, now tossed to the back of her head and no longer shielding her eyes from the view out the window. She stared, unseeing, as she traced through recent memories, searching for any possible clue. A red flag as to why the love of her life didn't think getting married today was worth his time or effort.

There was nothing. Not one moment of indecision. If anything, Jarred had been the one driven to make this day happen. He was the one who wanted the big church wedding with all the gaudy trimmings. All she wanted was Jared and a ring.

Something must have happened. Her heart gave way to the emptiness inside as silent tears ruined her professionally done makeup.

Locked behind the dressing room door, she gathered her thoughts and emotions. Having booted everyone from the room, the whispers from the other side of the barrier drifted through. The whispers were inevitable, but she couldn't bear hearing their conjectures and well-meant consolations.

Her temper flared. How dare he leave her alone to face this … this ungodly embarrassment? He'd better already be dead, because if she got her hands on him right now, well, she didn't know what she'd do. But she couldn't fathom any excuse that would ever compensate for not showing up. Good God. If he wasn't man enough to face her, the least he could have done was call her cell phone.

A gentle knock pulled her back to reality. She wasn't ready to face anyone. "Go away."

"Shelby, honey, it's mom. Please let me in."

Her mother meant well, but how could a woman who'd been raised with a gilded hand and sheltered her whole life help her now? She swallowed a sob and didn't respond.

Through the sparkling window glass, she watched spring prairie grasses bend and sway in the gentle morning breeze. The pasture behind the rectory bloomed with all the usual Dakota wild flowers. The heartier Indian paintbrush seemed to overtake the more fragile Jacob's ladder and pink Creeping Jenny. Yes, everything outside looked normal. Maybe she should be out there, riding her mare, instead of hiding in the bride's dressing room entrenched in an unbride-like pity party.

She looked around the well-appointed bridal suite. The walls seemed to come toward her like some Hollywood movie. She leaned forward in the white wicker chair, pushed the window sash open, and rested her cheek on the sill. *Just breathe.* The whispers on the other side of the door continued.

Not yet ready to talk to anyone, she refilled her champagne flute, grateful her attendants had left the magnum in the room an hour earlier when the Prelude had begun to play. The voices beyond the door grew quiet, then murmurs and gasps filtered through.

What? Had he finally showed? He'd better have a damned good reason for being this late.

A woman's voice broke the silence. "No!"

Her vision clouded and her pulse raced. Was that Jenny? Jared's mother? The woman's cries turned to whimpers, and Shelby could no longer hear their words.

A resolute calm settled on her like a shroud. She drained the glass.

The knock sounded again, this time, a hesitant request for admission. "Shelby, it's Dad."

He'd never crowded her, ever. Unlocking the door now could only bring bad news. She gripped the arms of the wicker chair, her eyes darting from the scene out the window, to the door, and back.

"Shelby, this can't wait. Let me in."

Something told her that was the last thing she wanted to do. Her organza, Alençon lace gown rustled as she stood. Her satin heels lay on the floor beneath the open window, long forgotten. She padded barefoot over to the door. "Just you, Dad. Okay?"

"Yes, just me. No one else."

She positioned herself behind the door, but it wasn't about anyone seeing her. She just couldn't bear the look she knew she'd see in their eyes. Not yet. She slid the bolt open. Her dad stepped through quickly, then closed and relocked the door. She moved into his arms without thought and breathed in her father's familiar essence.

His arms held years of comfort. Way more than the occasional skinned knees and junior high broken hearts, but her daddy's arms now were barely familiar. He held her with an awkwardness that belied his role of truth, trust and knowledge.

He cleared his throat with an effort she'd never before known.

"Dad? What is it? You know something. Where's Jared?"

"Come, sit down."

The lump in her throat threatened to explode. "No, Dad, tell me now."

He pulled her into his arms the way he'd done when she was seven and their dog had been hit by a car. A sob escaped her trembling lips. "No. No. No. No. No. No. NO!"

He stood there, holding her, and let the pieces fall into place. Letting simple truth flow past unspoken words. Words she wasn't ready to hear.

She gasped. "I need to go to him."

"No, honey. You can't. Not right now. We'll go later."

"Where is he?"

"Come." He guided her back to the white wicker chair. "Jared rode out early this morning to check on a couple cows. He knew one in particular was about to drop her calf and she'd always had a hard time." A heavy sigh blew across the top of her head as he held her in his arms. "His horse found its way home, saddled but without his rider."

She pulled back and looked into her father's eyes. "We have to go look for him! He could be out there, hurt. That horse would never run off like that. Jared's ridden him too long for that to happen." She ripped off her veil, turned her back to him, and lifted her hair. "Unzip me, I have to change."

Her father's hands stilled her frantic attempts to undress. "It's no use. The hired man found Jared out on the prairie near the old Miller place. It was too late. Nothing could be done."

She stared up at her father. He couldn't be saying these things. Not now. Not on her wedding day? Her father's voice broke into her thoughts, again.

"Remember the cow he'd found last winter, the one that almost died because a sheet of ice covered her face? Well, that cow went plumb loco trying to birth her calf. Looks like Jared had gotten a rope on the calf's feet, but he never got the chance to pull the calf."

Silence filled the room. She couldn't think. She couldn't talk.

"But there's more. Jared's body was trampled. That cow must have taken him right after he got down off his horse."

Her father's words faded to an echo and her vision tunneled into a grey mist. She couldn't feel her legs. With ice cold hands, she steadied herself against her father. She closed her eyes, remembering the last moments she and Jared had shared, the look in his eyes, as he'd told her good night.

"Sheriff Johnson said the coroner will release the body as soon as he can. It's pretty clear what happened." He hugged her again. "We'll take things one step at a time. Right now, you have to make some decisions."

She spun around to face him. "What are you talking about?" Tears flowed down her cheeks, unrestrained. "His mom and dad will be making the arrangements, not me. I never made it to 'wife'."

"I'm sure they'll want you involved. But, right now, we have a church full of people who loved you both. They're waiting. What do you want to do?"

She blinked. "I can't look at anyone, Dad. How can you ask me to do that?"

"Look honey, I know you're hurting and you haven't had time to absorb any of this. But think of Jared's parents. Gabe almost ran out of here when he found out about Jared. He said he'd get his rifle and shoot that cow, but he was too late for that. Neither the cow nor her calf survived the birthing."

The look in her father's eyes mirrored her own grief. Grief that had yet to register. She wondered when, if ever, that might happen. Jared, *her* Jared. Gone. Forever.

Her father thumbed her chin upwards and she was forced to look into his eyes. "Jared's parents are beside themselves with grief. As his fiancée', you need to make the first move and you need to do it soon. Remember, this was *his* wedding day, too."

"I don't think I have it in me to face the congregation, let alone Gabe and Jenny."

"You do, honey. You just have to fight your way through your grief. It's the right thing to do."

She gazed back out the window. The pale pink wild roses were in bloom. She hadn't noticed them earlier. Was that a sign? Jared hated the thorny things, but he'd planted roses in his mom's garden because they were her favorite flower. Was he giving her strength, through a bit of pink foliage, to face life without him?

She stood erect and stiffened her spine, then turned back to her dad. "You've always said we never get anything worth having without a fight. Why do I feel like the war is already over yet the real fight still lies ahead?"

Sans veil, she walked down the aisle on her father's arm toward her fiancé's parents waiting with the minister near the altar. Afraid to look at the faces in the crowd, yet scared not to, she gained strength as she moved up the aisle. Women dabbed at tears with pink and yellow tissues. Too bothered to mess with tissues, men snuffled and sniffed into their sleeves.

Gabe and Jenny drew her into a hug that bordered on a fierce denial of truth. The whispered words and phrases among the three of them would not be shared, but she allowed her heart to bleed along with theirs. Time stood still as they held onto each other. Finally, she turned to face the congregation. She cleared the lump from her throat, once again.

"This day is very sad." She looked heavenward, and then started again. "No, it's beyond sad. I can't begin to put my feelings into words, but I'm glad you're all here with us today." Her voice cracked, but she pushed on. "Given that, I will not allow this day to pass without us remembering what a wonderful man Jared Hanson is. . .um, I'm sorry." Her gaze dropped to the bride-white aisle runner and practiced the word, mentally. "Was."

Jenny's fingertips brushed her hand, and she gleaned strength through her fiancé's mom. "Let's not dwell on his death. Not right now. We all came here today to celebrate the union of two people who loved each other beyond all measure. So, let's do that." She raised her hand, joined with Jared's mother's hand, and forced a valiant smile.

"Please, join us in the reception hall. We will celebrate the life of a wonderful man, the love of my life."

Shelby stepped into the reception hall and the hired musicians began playing the song Jared had selected for the bride and groom's first dance. She froze. "How could they do this?"

Her father's face flushed, his lips compressed into a thin line. "Apparently, no one thought to inform the band. They weren't in the church, remember?" He pulled her into a protective hug. "Wait here, I'll fix this."

She held on to his arm. "No, stop. It's not their fault. You were right. I must see this through. If I can't do this now, I won't be able to handle the funeral—or anything else. Besides, Jared would want me to dance." She nodded toward the open floor. "The second dance is the father-daughter dance. Let's pretend that this is that song."

She felt all eyes on her as her father escorted her to the center of the parquet floor. He opened his arms, and she stepped into her father's embrace. Once around. Twice. Her mind spun back to when she was five and learning to dance from the tops of her daddy's boots.

Bits and fragments of heartfelt praise and condolence met her ears as they swirled past the crowded guest tables. The first verse barely ended when her brother tapped their dad's shoulder and her father stepped aside.

The top of Brice's head barely reached her shoulder, but he held her as if he was a mountain of a man. Strong, fierce, tender. Her chin quivered, and she gasped back a sob. His jaw tight, he never missed a step. A camera flashed. Someone was taking pictures. She sobbed again, but he held strong for them both.

Another tap on her partner's shoulder and her Grandpa Joe took her brother's place. She looked up onto his eyes, and she broke, again. His shoulders slumped and they held onto each other, swaying rather than stepping to the music. Her tears mixed with his as he hugged her through the next few bars.

The last strains of Jared's song found her staring into his father's eyes. Eyes so much like Jared's. Her arms encircled Gabe's neck, and together, they stood in the center of the hall, weeping openly as the last notes faded to silence.

Someone began to clap. Others joined in. She'd made it through the worst moments of her life. With friends and family so dear, somehow, she'd make it through whatever came next.

Born and raised on the Great Plains, Jaye Garland thrives on 'what-if' scenarios by turning ordinary ranch life events into novels steeped in adventure on the American West. Her award winning first novel, *The 25th Hour,* will be available in late July 2013.

My Mother and the Little House in the Swamp
How my mother, a strong Indian woman, got us here

Sanjay Fellini

The trip was worth it. In the summer of 1979, the parents had a plan and it started by luring my sister and I out of the blustering heat of our Bombay apartment and into to the dark air-conditioned coolness of the movies. I was only an impressionable young one, about eight years old and oblivious to the economic forces billowing around our very own house like a water cyclone. When my mother didn't join us, like she usually did, I didn't think anything about it, because she was dressed for work in her sparkling, freshly washed, white nursing uniform, a one piece miniskirt, *my* first sign that something was up. In India, *white* is an auspicious color---it's for funerals and shootouts in movies. Plus, Mum's odd excuse about why she was going to skip the movie (for a couple of extra shifts) felt tacked on, because she loved the extra hot samosas at the cinema halls as much as we did.

I knew she was joshing but why? Even though I had an uneasy feeling about leaving her behind, I waved goodbye as my father led my sister and me out the door and into the hustle and bustle of the busy Indian city streets.

I didn't see my mother again for three years. The spectacular movie we watched while she quietly packed her bags was called *Yadoon Ki Baraat*, a deceptively simple disco musical to the skinny street kids on the benches (the cheap seats) but a classic right wing comedy to the well dressed horde in the more expensive balcony seating.

Blame the cold war and Russia for the 'red' point of view but that's just the way the movies were back then. Not that the film was devoid of thrills. Early in *Yadoon*, the plucky Indian family with a longing for American style pants and short skirts instead of India dhoti's and Saris got what they deserved. Machine gunfire at a lavish outdoor birthday party. I saw the bloodbath coming a mile away when the entire cast showed up for the elegant affair dressed in spotless white—a dead giveaway that blood was going to follow. Sure enough, when the Cadillac stuffed with velveteen gangsters arrived shooting bullets, all the white saris, bell-bottoms and leisure suits got splattered in bright red blood.

And I was in movie heaven.

Luckily for India, the racy miniskirts and frantic disco beats lost the battle but won the war. Politics aside, I couldn't wait to run home and tell my mother about the excesses of western culture. When I finally got home to our modest, government approved high-rise for railway employees on a budget, I found an empty nest. And a funny feeling, called abandonment, replaced my movie high. Had the velveteen pimps from the movie we had just seen kidnapped our helpless Mum, in her nursing whites no less?

I tried to contain a paranoid fear welling up inside me. After calling out her name in all the squared off rooms that all looked the same, I turned to the one person in the house who had to know where she was—Papa. "Where's our mummy?" I casually asked him. If our mother was strapped to a bomb somewhere with seconds to live, I needed to know. "What have you done with her?"

Papa tried to make sense of it all and answered, truthfully. "She's gone to America," he informed us. "So that we can all have more money."

Gulp! It wasn't my imagination, *our* lives had tuned into a Bollywood movie. My own beautiful mother with the white stockings and the black eyeliner had been lured away from Indira Gandhi's slow road to heaven for all. She chose instead America's make-money-now, debt-ridden, supply-side economics of Uncle Sam. Course, I had tons of questions for him like: Was life really better there? Did people really have color TVs in every home? And more importantly, who was going to make our lunches and take us to school?

My sister, a couple years older than my 8, had been standing in the hallway and listening. She was not taking my mother's absence very well. She walked into the room, and from the look on her face, I could tell she was on the verge of losing it. Seconds later, when she threw up all over herself, my feelings were confirmed.

I turned to my father for guidance. Papa took a seat on a rattan chair by the square window and looked out into the courtyard. Mum was going to miss the Monsoons. I could feel the water in the air. "Your mother is on Air India flight 6762," he confessed, sharing my mother's itinerary. "She's going to New York City. Over there, she will meet with her sister, Elizabeth, and become a nurse. We will follow soon."

I don't know if I ever forgave her for leaving. Maybe that's why I'm still hooked on the movies. Back in our flat, I had more questions. Papa tried his best to answer. All I heard was *blah, blah, blah.* It was pretty devious come to think of it. While we were at the movies, having a gay old time, my mother had boarded an elegant 747 and joined the mass exodus of young Indian nurses bravely going into the unknown, also known as Brooklyn. Jumbo jets were leaving India at all hours with rows of young women munching on idli and sambar right from their silver dhabas, wondering if *Kentucky Fried Chicken* really deserved the reputation it was getting from returning vacationers, that is was a delicacy. For a meat eating Christian like my mother, the idea of frying a whole chicken in oil (very expensive in India) made the speculative journey to the west tolerable. Almost mythic.

Migration to the New World was effortless when compared to journeys made in the golden tinted days of the past, like in *The Little House on the Prairie*, a book about roughing it in the American pioneer days by Laura Ingalls. If we *had* lived in the Wild West, Mum would have needed her machete made of black iron for her journey, and not a passport. But in the summer of 1979, it wasn't like that. All she needed was her trusty stethoscope and a nursing license to relieve bronchitis and asthma or whatever made people sick in the 70s. Her favorite part of the whole nursing job was asking her patients to "inhale and cough" with her slightly English sounding, Bombay twang.

It wasn't all work. There was a brief sojourn for my mother in Queens, New York that could only be described as delightful. I know because she never stopped talking about it. In between all the shifts and the long distance phone calls, she got to be a teenager again with her girlfriends, other young nurses like her, boarding together, all shacked up in a two bedroom apartment, all of them working, saving, sending paychecks to the Bank of My Husband In India and spending the few hours that were their own in lines for hours on end, filling out thousands of applications that spawned miles of paper work, even through the toughest New York blizzards, with temperatures so low that the nurses turned into walking icicles. In the end, the work would be worth the effort. Back in India, there were hundreds, thousands of men and children waiting for visas and plane tickets to join their wives and mothers. Kids like us.

And so, that was how our mum, the nurse from Kerela, staked her claim in a brand New World and dragged her snot-nosed kids along to share in the bounty: a comfy couch in a suburban neighborhood, a five cup rice-maker by Ginsu, and hours of gut drenched television to savor.

As with a lot of stories about my parents, everything started out innocently enough. Mr. and Mrs. Mathews left India with bellbottoms and muttonchops. Mum had the muttonchops and Papa had the bell-bottoms. Once they got that confusing wardrobe mix-up straightened out, Mum became a registered nurse and Papa got a job at some factory down the street. To this day, I don't know what he did but I know he left the house each morning with a black lunchbox made of steel. A couple of months later, I couldn't believe it myself, but we were living the American Dream in upstate New York. The Catskills were on one side, our storybook town on the other and we were right smack in the middle.

New York City waited for us, if we dared to make the trip (only a hundred miles away by Greyhound). Yep, for a couple of bony, brown skinned kids from the crushing melee of a third world city in the 70s, it sure seemed like peacetime, until one blisteringly cold upstate winter, when snowdrifts and ice sheets coated everything for miles like a layer of shimmering permafrost on the land. I could smell change in the air, and it smelled like brake fluid.

At first I paid no attention to it. Besides, we had other more challenging issues at hand. My sister was ten and I was eight and we were dealing with our first great national tragedy. Dark-eyed Freddie Prinze, comedian and actor, star of *Chico & the Man*, had shot himself at the tender young age of twenty-two. We heard about our favorite comedian's distressing death on our parent's functional black and white television set that was proudly displayed on a wooden shelf inside the second floor bedroom of our upstate rental. Right next to a crucifix. The news reports were grim, and my sister Mini was not taking it well. Like most of the country, she was in love with Chico. So was I, as a matter of fact. While I internalized my pain, she needed a pat on the back, and I was the only one around.

"Will God take Chico to heaven?" she innocently wondered in my direction, asking the question everyone with a UHF signal had on his or her lips. I shrugged. Suicide was an unforgivable sin, and as far as the Catholic Church was considered, Chico was going straight to hell. How was I supposed to know anyway?

The only thing I knew for sure was that I could not suffer through another moment of her non-stop sniffles so I said, "Chico went to heaven in a golden elevator."

"Really," she cried, allowing herself to feel only *so much* better.

I stopped her before she went into full-on mourning, complete with bubbling mucus and tears–all part of her healing process. Even though I, too, was heartbroken, I did my best to stay dry. Unlike her, I was already a private child, prone to crying in the bathroom or a bedroom, behind locked doors, afraid of letting people see my tears. Not my sister, she blubbered in public any chance she could get.

And I had to keep it together because my time-challenged parents were running late, as usual. They were on I.P.T., or Indian People's Time – always about eleven hours behind schedule for the continental U.S. but right on time in Kerala.

For once, I needed them and as usual, they were nowhere to be found. It wasn't just Chico's early exit. I had reason to be worried. Papa was out teaching Mum how to drive, which was the equivalent of a blind person judging a beauty contest. Like a lot of Asian women, Mum wasn't meant to drive anything. Actually, if you asked my father, he would say that she was meant to drive people crazy. Still, *she* was out there, in the frigid snow, working towards her drivers license and keeping my dad's gigantic Malibu in one lane – an impossible task for her lead foot and devil-may-care attitude toward speed limits, but a stand out combination when trying to flatten people like pancakes.

Because I was stressing, I left my sister by the portable sized TV, went to the window and checked the horizon for my parents. And strangely enough, like a furry white rabbit out of a magician's hat, my dad's American made, cream colored Buick, our first car, appeared out of nowhere, careening down the street and headed for our two-story rental building. And us. I opened the window and, sure enough, I got smacked in the face with the stench of brake fluid wafting in the ether. It had to be coming from their car. There was also an ear-piercing scream, like someone was trying to wrestle control of the wheel. Probably Papa.

That made sense, because my mother had her foot on the gas and hated to be ordered around. I held my breath and braced for a scene out of an action movie. "Duck," I screamed in my sister's direction. From what I could gather, we had about thirty seconds before we took a direct hit. I could not let that happen. Wonder Woman was on TV later that night, my all time favorite lady outside of my mother. Dead or alive, I was not going to miss it. With my night television plans locked in my head, I grabbed my sister and we threw ourselves behind the shelf, closed our eyes and waited for a white tunnel to fall from the ceiling and take us into the Pearly Gates.

One moment, it sounded like the car was down the street, and then, we heard it disappear under the house and crash with a thunderous bang of metal eating wood. After the immense sound of the collision, there was a menacing quiet. In the stillness, I ran to the other room, stepped onto the veranda and saw a ghastly sight – the steely front end of the General Motors car was chomping up part of the house, like a mechanical land shark out of water.

No sign of the parents. "Mummy! Papa," I screamed. So did my sister. From what I could see, there was nothing coming from the car. Were they alive? Dead? I had to know? I ran down the stairs as fast as I could, and when I got the driveway, I found them alive and barely moving, in shock. Mum was still behind the wheel wearing her best *'it wasn't me'* look of wonder on her face. I would have done the same. From my childlike point of view, taking a two-story house off its foundation was pretty darn impressive, but in the world of adults, not necessarily a good thing. I could not see my dad, but I knew he was screaming. All I could think about was how much punishment would my mother would get ... a week, a year? Maybe two years in solitary confinement with extra hard labor?

I called out to them. "Are you guys okay?"

Both of them were too stunned to answer. And there was a thick cloud of smoke coming out of the hood so they could not see me either. After another moment that felt like eternity, or two Indian movies back to back, Papa quickly extinguished the quiet, threw his creaky passenger side door open and carefully got out, one foot at a time, to inspect the carnage. His feet, circa India 1933, were not made for ice. They were made for dirt roads made of red mud in Kerala, the southern-most state in India and his home. Two steps later, he lost his balance, slipped and fell into a sneaky snowdrift about three feet tall that was right behind him, forcing him to curse in Malayalam.

Translation: "BAD SNOW! BAD SNOW!"

My sister laughed from her perch on the Veranda. So did I. Despite my giddy laughing, we all had *reason to worry*. As a *fresh off the plane* family, it was our second auto-crash in the span of a few months. My mother had already crashed the very same car at the local Safeway the week before – and almost killed me in the process. That time, I hit the dashboard and busted a tooth. But it wasn't all bad, I got a pint of vanilla ice cream in exchange for my pain and suffering and a lot of over-the-top crying out of Mum when she threw herself to the ground and beat her chest in agony. (Showing off her crying skills, I suppose) In fact, with all the smash-ups going around, I was certain my parents got their driver's licenses out of a gumball machine at the local Woolworth's next to the penny operated Merry-Go-Round. Not that staying in her lane or keeping ten feet away from every other car on the road would help my mother. The woman wasn't getting it. She was a danger to the public and homes framed in wood.

Outside, in chilly snow, Mum refused to accept her role in the crash and get out of the busted Malibu leaking bile colored fluid and sickly gray smoke into the sky. That would not happen until she paused for a second and realized that she may have killed one of her own in the hubbub. When that terrible thought crossed her mind, she threw open her car door, fell onto her knees, and released a piercing wail, "Where are my children?", into the afternoon.

My sister and I did not respond. Not *right away,* anyway. We held onto the wonderful moment as long as we could, waiting to see what she would do next. We were in luck. Mum continued to vent, this time, acting all dramatic, like a woman in a Greek tragedy starring Katherine Hepburn. Anything was better than having to fess up that she should not be trusted behind the wheels of a car – maybe a buggy, or a golf cart – but nothing that required any kind of eye hand coordination and empathy for passersby and their pets.

After she was done beating her chest for five whole minutes and breaking all her bangles in the process, I pushed aside a piece of wreckage, ran up to her, and released her from her guilt. "I'm right here," I yelled, over her wailing. She turned to me to and started to cry when she realized I was real flesh and blood and not a vision. "Chico saved us from you," I screamed, wanting to honor the Mexican American Hero and give credit where it was due. "We were watching him die on TV when you ran into the house."

"I'm alive, too," my sister blurted, still up on the veranda, sobbing away, and kind of throwing a wet blanket on the whole situation. "Mummy, the 'Hunk-a-Rican' is dead."

"Oh praise Jesus," my mother bellowed, throwing herself to the ground, deftly avoiding the giant hole she had busted into our apartment building and the "why me" expression on my father's face. Papa didn't know what to do so he just stood there gaping. Wanting to disappear. Even though we were clearly okay, Mum could not waste an opportunity to show what a dramatist she could be, given the right circumstances. That's why she fell onto the ice and started rolling around, screaming in pain, kind of like a person on fire would do. *Stop, drop, and roll* is what it's called in books at school and at Fire Stations everywhere. I don't know what Mum called it, probably *when all else fails.* But there she was, on the frost-covered tundra of the front yard, making retarded snow angels, while my sister, my father and I waited for her to run her batteries down.

Luckily, that was the end of the ice age for us. After taking the house off its hinges, Mum did not get punished, but had had enough with New York. "A

God fearing family from India deserves sun," she cried. My father agreed. Without consulting the kids, they quickly packed up everything we had into the wrecked car and moved the family to the balmy suburbs of Houston, Texas. After a brief stay in temporary housing, and a shady apartment complex near the city, my parents hit the burbs in style with their ranch style home, not too far from the Gulf of Mexico. Thanks to Mum, it was a terrific existence, and exactly what we had dreamed of back in Bombay. We had it all, a brick-covered cottage, a somewhat dried up patchwork lawn in green strung together like a furry Lego set, a sprinkler that sprang into action three times every day, and a happy starter Oak in the middle of the somewhat messy yard.

As far as survival was concerned, the bumper-car period of our lives had ended without a massive body count, just some missing teeth (on my part) and a fear of merging traffic that would plague me for the rest of my life. But like I said, it could have been worse. Papa let Mummy get a compact Chevy she could park (and that also doubled as a purse), and she got him a nifty gadget called a microwave oven that kept him busy for hours, but only for a few convenient minutes at a time. And best of all, Mummy finally got her hands on some real, honest to goodness Southern Fried Chicken, plump and golden fried, and suddenly, the rest of her life magically fell into place.

Sanjay Fellini, a.k.a. Benjamin Mathews, was born in Bombay and moved to the US as a child. As one of a handful of South East Asians in a rough-and-tumble Texas high school, Benny tried his best to assimilate. As if that wasn't enough for a sensitive sixteen year old, Benny was also coming to terms with a severe case of Cinemania. Hooked on movies, Benny became the quintessential filmmaker and writer. A young man whose ideal day included sitting through three or more movies back to back to back, one would assume Benny to be a maudlin, tragic literary figure, prone to excruciating bouts of self-pity and remorse. *Au contraire*, he is a hopeless romantic with a sharp eye for the absurd. His engaging voice and unique experiences resonate with anyone who has felt alone in a crowd or overwhelmed by the mischievous forces of Fate.

Some Mothers are Not Perfect

In which my mother's fear of other females affects my ability to make friends

Sanjay Fellini

In sixth grade, I found myself drawn to a bright-eyed Jody Foster lookalike with strawberry-blonde tresses affectionately named Hildy. She was the girl who sat at the back of the school bus and let the boys feel her up, under her t-shirt and *even in the most private of places,* under her bra. Yes, her behavior was majorly distressing, but something about the way she went on with the rest of her school day with a slightly faded grin, *despite* her morning mauling, made me want to latch onto her for dear life. My mother, being the untamed, reckless *Elephant Indian Mother* she was, did not take kindly to my oddball selection in the BFF department. Right away, she sensed something was amiss with the girl from nowhere in particular who seemed to materialize out of thin air into my life. Spells were cast. Bombs were thrown. Threats were made. Yet, I did not give up my pursuit of a female costar. After I begged and pleaded, my mother said I could hang out with Hildy, on one condition: the "crazy white girl" was not allowed inside our house. Or else!

At the time, I believed my mother was a racist, but now I know the truth. She wanted to be the only woman in my life. And to label my mother in puffy white nursing shoes *a racist* is not fair. *David Duke in a sari she was not.* To be a racist you have to have bone-crushing power over the people you can't stand, and poor old Mum, a typical Indian nurse, one of many who came from India to fill an American nursing shortage in the 70s, was powerless over everyone except my sister and me.

Suspicious, is a better word for her fear of Hildy. When I asked Mum about it, she said it was "white folks" that worried her most—which was kind of strange, because Texas was *white people* central. Only a foreign country like Sweden or Norway could be more whitewashed. But I have to admit it—I reveled in her badness. Hating "the blue-eyed devil," gave her anti-establishment street 'cred' which made her way cool and mixed up at the same time *and* rather unpredictable. Anytime I was lying around the house without a thing to do, which happened more than I'd like to believe, I liked to imagine that our sari clad mother had a potent back story, that she had spent many years in inner city college as the hip girlfriend to several *Black Panthers*, and that's why she feared *the man,* although, in reality, I have to concede that Mum was probably more *Al Sharpton* in a sari than the *Bride of Malcolm X.*

At least, for her sake, Mum wasn't obvious about her weirdness. No GOD HATES WHITEY t-shirts or posters around our house. At work, she got along just fine with the white nurses on her floor, even passed around her *to-die-for* chicken curry like a peace pipe at their once a week potlucks. Her stand-out curry worked double time – first, as a delicious food ambassador, and second, as a fantastic, in a flash, one-dish meal from the *golden age* of casseroles, the 1970s. For her selfless generosity, Mum never left an office party empty-handed. She returned to her famished brood with mouthwatering strawberry and grape flavored gelatin molds, buttery scalloped potatoes cooked with succulent meats, sublime *Green Goddess* salads, refreshing sherbets in green, orange and yellow, served in tall frosted glasses with a Sprite. These recipes soothed her troubled soul and added a little fizz to our mundane, suburban existence. A sweet trade if you ask me.

Unfortunately, none of her work parties ended in a scuffle with my mom being led out in handcuffs for calling someone a *damned Yankee,* or even worse, the whore offspring of *imperialist pigs.* If she *had* gotten into trouble with the police, at least then, I might have been more popular in school for having a mother in the pokey. Guess her *badness* was like my entire high school experience, a wasted opportunity.

Okay so back to Hildy When I actually tried to bring my new best friend into the house, Mum tried to build a force field around me made of hot curry. The more she resisted the more I wanted Hildy. When I just plain asked her why she could not come into my room, she predictably flew into a violent rage. "You cannot be cavorting with a dirty white girl!" she screamed. "I did not bring you all the way from India for some ill mannered white girl to have her way with you."

With those words, Mum confirmed my worst fears, that her brain had been sucked out and reprogrammed by Luis Farrakhan.

"What if she wanted to use the restroom?"

"No."

"What if she wanted to call you aunty?"

"Oh no."

Mum shook her head and said, "All your fun has to happen on the front porch or on the street." Not a problem, I foolishly thought, believing the stinking porch went on forever and wasn't like all the other porches, about two feet wide and twenty feet long. Once Hildy and I started using the porch as our playground, summer killed our plans, fast. Pretty soon, in torrid triple digit weather, we were sweating up, trying to play board games in the midst of a sweltering heat wave. To prevent overheating, we ran to our foot tall kiddie pool made of blue plastic, deep enough to soak our feet during the hottest part of the day. Despite the boiling weather and my gentle pleading, Hildy couldn't cool off in the pool with me, end of story. When Hildy insisted on splashing around, Mum said I had to get out, or else.

Nothing made sense to me, but then again, I was trying to make sense of my mother. When I asked why, Mum said she was preventing a dangerous cross contamination of Hildy's 'white' germs. I said "HAAAAAAAAAA?" and Mum said, "That's the way it is going to be around our house."

It was apartheid, plain and simple. Instead of running off in a huff of anger, like I wanted to, Hildy bravely stuck it out, and in the end, we ended up the better pals because of it. But for my mother sake, we did as she ordered and kept our afternoon rendezvous within the limits of the porch until that one fateful afternoon, when our rules of engagement took a free fall. It happened during a game of Operation (by Milton Bradley). Mum was in the kitchen making her favorite south Indian fish curry. Hildy and I were on the porch, lying flat on our bellies, with our feet in the air, playing a game, making the most of a Saturday. Halfway into our third game, Hildy came up with a wild idea.

"Let's become best-selling writers," she said, like it was no big deal.

"Sure," I replied, wanting to be as supportive as possible and make up for my mother's odd behavior. Truth be told, when you're a kid, nothing's too crazy, even writing a bestseller on a porch in the sun. To prove that I was on her team, I ran inside the house and fetched what I assumed were the supplies of an award winning writing team: some paper, a pen, a bottle of white out and a rope to hang ourselves when we actually had to read out loud what we had written down. While I was inside the house looking for supplies, Hildy did her best to wait on the porch. It was tough going. There was a moment when she came close to coming inside, eyes bulging like a hiker looking over the edge of a deep canyon. When I barreled out of my room, with my hands full, I pulled her away, before my mother noticed and we settled down on the porch again, and got started.

"It's important to get everything down on paper," she said, as she started to write, with a faraway look in her eyes that I misread as pensive. After thinking for an hour, and not writing a word, I did my best to not let the emptiness of blank pages get me down.

"What do you have in mind, anyway?" I asked eagerly, knowing it was her idea in the first place. I resisted going back to the Operation game, which suddenly seemed so yesterday in my eyes, compared to co-authoring a hit book and going cross country on a book tour.

"Let's write a V. C. Andrews book," she said at the start. "Only our story would be about a girl named Bobby." The Molotov cocktail natures of her troubles were laid out for me, bit by bit, a chapter at a time.

"Are you Bobby?" I asked. Despite having a "Facts of Life" level of understanding of the teenage mind, I was not about to fall for that third grade psychology trick, until she convinced me otherwise.

"No, "she assured me, with a hand over her left breast, "Bobby is not me," she assured me again as her voice rose.

To make myself look more like a writer, I put my pencil behind my ear, like I'd seen writers do on TV to appear as scholarly as possible and did my best to not let the dramatic juices get cramped up inside me. It must have been the wise look on my face or the pencil because Hildy started to unleash hitherto unknown details about her life that neither one of us, without advanced degrees in psychology and a lot more living, were prepared to deal with.

Hours later, rooted to the same spot, I got a nagging feeling in my prefrontal cortex that the not-so-merry best-seller was about her—just like I had suspected. The story started innocently enough. First, there was a nontoxic early chapter on how 'Bobby' wanted to go into fashion merchandising, also known to writers worldwide as character development. And then it got gruesome, fast. I found out that 'Bobby' had a creepy father that would have been right at home as the bad guy in the complete works of V. C. Andrews, especially the *Flowers in the Attic* series. Bobby's father was "touchy feely" in a bad way.

I didn't speak up. I was twelve. Hildy was my first white friend, and I wanted to sneak her inside the house, someday, despite my crazy mother. And besides, she swore up and down on our hallowed porch, that she was not Bobby. So, like a good friend, I didn't bug her with questions. The whole time we were writing, Mum must have been in her kitchen listening to us having a great time, getting spooked. The moment she officially decided to go ballistic, Hildy and I were taking a much-needed break from writing *her* memoirs and working off some steam in a heated game of *Operation*. After I had pulled out my favorite piece of organ meat, the plastic heart, it was Hildy's turn.

"*No biggie!*" she said. Like all the other times we played together, Hildy got up and went about the mundane task with her usual panache. She wanted to show me she was not only an up and coming writer but that she had a future as a surgeon. That has to be why she ended up precariously balanced on one knee while trying to pull out the puny kidney resting inside the game without setting off the obnoxious buzzer.

Not an easy task, in hospitals or on porches in the Deep South. In fact, she so lost her concentrated effort, that I could see balls of clear sweat well up on her forehead, pull away from her skin, and hit the game board like huge gumdrops.

"Hildy," I remarked. "You better be careful, you might get electrocuted."

That's when Mum, smelling of fish curry masala and fear, barreled out of the house in one of her furious, over-the-top rages, and kicked the board game into the sky, sending the whole thing, Hildy, the tweezers, all the fake little plastic organs, and most importantly, my summer friendship, to the stratosphere. Despite everything, my only friend in the entire Milky Way Galaxy remained calm. Without erupting in a geyser of red-hot anger, one that was well-deserved considering the circumstances, Hildy showed us how evolved she was. Like Gandhi, in the Richard Attenborough's movie, she took the non-violent way out of a major, unprecedented jam. She quietly got up, wiped her hands on her hips, shoved her bare feet into her dark green *Hush Puppies,* pulled her strawberry blonde strands of hair back into a waiting scrunchie, and walked off into the future without saying a word.

Mum, went back inside. And I lost a true friend and possible best-selling authoress.

Every day after that, I looked for her mop of dirty blonde hair on the porch, but she never returned. Weeks later, a new semester of school began, and I slowly but surely forgot the whole episode. The book was dead. So were the good times on the porch. Needless to say, Mum was pleased with her impersonation of a human hurricane. Once again, I made excuses for her chaotic *borderline bananas* behavior. Maybe she was raging because she and my father slept in different rooms. Maybe she wanted to torture me because she *despised him* so much. Maybe she had too much red chili in her fish masala. Despite her hellacious actions, I resolved to love her to death anyway. It's not like I had a choice. She was my biological mother after all.

Every once in a while, when she was in one of her good moods and lying spread eagle on the couch, my sister and I would climb onto her wide lap and nuzzle on her like two little kittens, purring the whole time. And about her fear of the blue- eyed-devil? Time fixed that glitch. Years later, when my sister eloped with a delightful young white man from St. Louis, Mum finally got over her fear of the Nordic races, but, sadly, not soon enough for me to salvage my friendship with a delicate girl named Hildy.

When I actually tried to get down to the gritty details about what caused her weekend *bigotry,* I decided to check out some movies about India before Independence to figure out where she went off the rails, and I discovered a clue to my mother's illness in Richard Attenborough's *Academy Award winning* film entitled *Gandhi.* After viewing the epic film about social injustice on a massive scale, I swiftly placed the blame on the British Raj for my mother's *fear and loathing* of *the blue eyed devil.* Back in India, before independence, the whole disgusting Imperialistic Raj thing was no picnic for anyone of color, which was the *whole freaking country,* I might add.

After independence, with the help of the movies, there was some healing. 'Can we get along' became a way of life for the nation. Cut to twenty-five years later, the 70s, India's movie golden age. Because the filmmakers could not hate on each other, the only people left to demonize were the white men and women who played the token baddies in the films of 'Bollywood.' Film producers, who knew what their audiences wanted, raided the beaches, sand dunes, and drum circles for left over hippy-types for the whiteness of their skin, because they could do what most self-respecting Indian actors could not do: become a general nuisance.

These hippies were the furthest thing from the British Foreign Policy run amok possible and the very definition of unsuspecting. Instead of world domination, these innocent travelers were lured to India for the exchange rate, the promise of free grass, cheap digs, utter salvation, and ashrams filled with sex. When they had tired of life on beaches, they were lured into the movies, into bit parts that made them the butt of the jokes: A stray Australian could play an evil British soldier, foaming at his mouth. A sweet faced Norwegian women could play a floozy in a revealing bikini who thickened the plot by kissing decent Indian men who should have been home with their wives and not chasing her decadent shimmy.

After watching a couple of films from this psychedelic era, Pappa naturally believed all white women were easy and sinful. And Mum believed every man wanted to rape her, and that the white woman was a She Devil who wanted to break up her happy home, mate with her husband, throw her into a prison work camp, and, even worse, send her innocent children to an inexpensive junior college for a worthless associates degree. Basically, there was no escaping this escapist diatribe. Because of her diet of movies, it only made sense that Mum insisted that I ditch the diabolical white girl femme fatale the movies of India had warned her about, and go Indian.

New Life

Patti Macdonald

The subject backed the fancy Black Onyx Lexus LX out of the garage and jerked to a stop. Glancing over her shoulder to check for traffic, she froze in place.

My heart sped up as I flipped down the visor and slouched behind the steering wheel of my dingy gray Caravan. Surely she hadn't seen me?

Usually I hated being short and nondescript. This was one of the times it paid off. Those features I detested, being middle aged and unobtrusive, were the very characteristics needed for my Agency job. While I'd hated being described as mousy when I was growing up, I now considered it praise. No one ever described me accurately.

Those characteristics ensured I met my employers' objectives. It meant sufficient money in my checking account and even more in my offshore account. I received double payments: one for IRS purposes, the other for mine. It was the perfect setup except for one thing. I wanted to retire.

"There's no such thing as retiring." My boss had stated as I signed the contract. I'd laughed at the time, thinking he was joking. His words ricocheted in my memory as I followed my subject.

But contracts were made to be broken, or at least modified. I wanted whatever was left of my life back. The Agency was selfish, sucking the life from its employees. And even then, they wouldn't release anyone. Rumors spread about employees who'd escaped, but the rumors were never confirmed. Confirmation meant death.

The female subject snarled something at the two toddlers buckled into fancy car seats in the back as she waited for a green light. The kids shouldn't have caused her trouble, not with the twin video screens built into the headrests in front of them. Apparently her employer didn't pay her enough to deal with the devil's spawn.

She turned the vehicle into the parking lot attached to the medical center and headed toward the parking garage. I followed at a non-threatening distance and parked a couple of spaces down from her. She rushed the toddlers from the car and dragged them along toward the building. When one of the toddlers tripped and began wailing, she yanked him to his feet and pulled him along in her wake. His screams echoed against the others cars in a cacophony of pain. It was all I could do to stay buckled in place. But once their pediatrician appointments were over, no one would come looking for them for a while.

"Everything changes for the better." Yeah, that was another of my boss's platitudes. He was wrong. After forty years, my life hadn't improved enough.

I'd gone passively along with whatever the Agency wanted from me. It had been a one way street. Sure, I could change the direction of the sign, but better still to move somewhere nobody could find me. I glanced down at the oversized shirt that covered my newly constructed curves. The box of hair coloring waited for me in my by-the-week apartment. Tomorrow everyone would be looking for a nondescript middle aged woman. Tomorrow, as I boarded my flight to Italy, I'd wear a curve-hugging black knit dress that nicely contrasted with my red hair. Tomorrow, I'd slip on my red-soled heels. Tomorrow I'd leave my old self behind and hold on tight to the passport with my new picture and new name.

Her routine was predictable. The nanny would shove the children into their car seats and take off. The next stop would be the mall for ice cream and toys. Too bad they'd miss out on the ice cream.

I thought about the toys tucked into my bag, the toys they'd begged her for last week. I'd ordered them online so I wouldn't get my fingerprints on the packaging. Let the Agency go on a wild goose chase while I made my escape.

The toddlers would only be in my possession for a short time, just long enough to pass them on to my contact. Within a week, they'd have new names along with new parents. The children were the fortunate ones. That woman, not so much. She didn't know that once her life ended, mine could begin.

Seasons of Exile

Stella Sinclair

Smyrna, Asia Minor, September, 1922

Petra and Marina's safety hinged on the old widow disguises they wore. If the disguises failed, their fate would be worse than Petra could imagine. She'd been warned. She crossed herself, praying that the approaching Turkish soldier wouldn't realize she and Marina were young women. With a shudder, she reached for her niece's cold, damp hand and pulled Marina even closer behind the single barrel. Her thighs cramped from sitting on her heels. She tucked their skirts tight about their bodies. They clung to each other.

She held her breath, in fear and against the stench in the alley. The pungent odor of rotting, abandoned food in looted homes made her eyes water. At least, she hoped it was food, and not bodies, in the homes. Petra bit her lower lip at the thought of dead Greek bodies in the empty houses.

Crack! His horse stomped a glossy hoof on the cobbled stones, ebony tail carried high like a banner. In the small alley surrounded by rows of two-story rock buildings, the sound reminded Petra of her brother-in-law's rifle when he went hunting. Marina flinched against Petra's body. She squeezed her niece's hand, as if a squeeze could reassure the younger teen against her fear of the Turkish soldier.

Petra averted her gaze to the horse so the man wouldn't feel her watching him. Deep breaths inflated the horse's body beneath a chestnut coat that shimmered from fastidious grooming. What kind of people valued horses above humans? Sides heaving, it stood still, awaiting the soldier's next command. Petra's hatred for the soldier sent waves through her body.

Why did he stop so suddenly in the alley? She hazarded a glance at the soldier again. His attention was riveted on something in front of him, toward the left. Her breath caught in her throat. Could he sense their presence?

She recognized the uniform from the newspaper. He was one of the Lancers of the Imperial Guard. One of the feared Turkish soldiers she'd heard so much about. While his interest was elsewhere, she studied him. Gold buttons glittered on the scarlet chest piece of the Turkish soldier's royal blue tunic, and his fez was a truncated felt cone of the same royal blue.

Almost imperceptibly, the rider tapped the horse's side with a gleaming black boot. Petra's gaze followed the boots upwards. A black and gold-trimmed scabbard rested on his leg. At the thought of what rested in the scabbard, she shivered. In response to the soldier's boot, the horse took several steps forward.

A young woman! He'd approached a young woman who stared at him. Petra could hear her praying in Armenian. She was dressed in the finery Petra saw when she passed the Armenian Church on many Sundays. A white blouse and scarlet skirt. The young woman trembled so that the clinking of gold and silver coins adorning her multicolored headpiece echoed faintly in the desolate alley. The combination of her muttered prayers and clinking coins accompanied the snorting breaths of the horse, bouncing off the walls and hanging in the fetid air.

Petra remained crouched in complete stillness, breath held, her black-clad arms tight around Marina. A tiny bead of sweat formed on Petra's forehead, right above her temple, irritating and tickling her skin. She twitched her eye. She dared not reach for it. The soldier might notice the movement. The droplet slid down insidiously, daring her to reach up. She closed her right eye. Maybe this would redirect its path. Then she contorted her face. The blasted drop of perspiration continued its subtle downfall. Petra clenched her neck as it trickled down, stealing a glimpse at the quivering Armenian woman who still stared at the soldier.

"You dare look at me, impertinent intruder." The soldier's thick black mustache curved up. Waxed and artificial, its points enhanced the menacing scowl that distorted his features.

The young woman's trembling intensified. Her eyes, brown like roasted cocoa beans from the Ivory Coast, opened so wide that they were ringed in white. She didn't take her eyes away from his frightening visage, in spite of his warning. Look away, look away. Petra prayed for the maiden to cast her eyes elsewhere.

The dark-skinned soldier unsheathed his saber. A hiss accompanied its effortless egress. It flashed in the sunlight. Marina pushed her face into Petra's shawl. Petra held her close, but kept watching. Against her shoulder, Petra felt Marina turn her attention back to the confrontation, and then away again.

He raised his curved saber. Petra held her breath. Then he shook his head and returned the weapon to its scabbard.

Petra exhaled silently. Her relief turned to horror as he raised his other arm, revealing the lance. The banner affixed just below the lance's blade was filthy with blood. Petra gulped the lump wedged in her throat.

Casually, the Turkish soldier leaned back in his saddle. He plunged the lance into the maiden's stomach. With a loud whoosh, the young woman's air expelled from her lungs. Petra clamped her mouth over a cry. The blade exited right below the maiden's waist-length hair. As he removed the lance, the soldier twisted his arm and whooped. The glee on his face frightened Petra more than his earlier scowl.

Blood poured out of the young woman's abdomen. She slumped to the cobbled street. Petra averted her gaze from the soldier, afraid to be found guilty of staring at him. Hooves on the cobbled street signaled his departure.

She chanced a look at the maiden's body, now lying in the street. Crimson covered what might have been her special occasion attire, and a trickle of blood escaped her lips. So much blood. The crevices between the stones in the street pooled with the maiden's blood streaming from her body.

An alley cat skulked toward the nearest rivulet and lapped. Stomach roiling, Petra turned her head, afraid to shoo the opportunistic feline for fear of attracting the attention of the departing soldier.

She spied the open door of an abandoned storefront nearby. Heart pounding, she led a silent, weeping Marina through the open doorway, around the vandalized merchandise scattered about, and up the winding staircase. Slouched by a window, Petra watched as more Turkish soldiers thundered past, horses neighing and snorting as their hooves thundered on the cobblestone.

She wiped Marina's tears from her face. For every tear Petra wiped, two flowed where one had been. She embraced her niece. The streets, which had not been busy before the attack, were now empty. All inhabitants, Greek and Armenian, sought haven from a feared onslaught.

Why did she disobey Dimítri's instructions? Her brother-in-law, Marina's father had carefully planned their evacuation from the city. He warned them about venturing out in public, told them to stay in the house. But she didn't. And now she and Marina were in peril. It was all her fault. Curse her impulsive heart. Eva was right. She was rash and inconsiderate of others. Eva, her sister and Dimítri's wife, had told her she was selfish. Now it seemed she was right.

She risked her own and Marina's life to find a copy of her college transcript. To prove she'd gone to school. Petra clenched her fists to keep her frustration from coming out.

A flicker of movement caught her peripheral vision. She glanced left. A Greek flag, unattached to a pole, glided upon the sea's breeze. Tattered, bloody, and charred, the flag drifted downward. Like Petra's spirits. The flag's fate was now suspended, determined by the fickleness of a treacherous breeze, like the fate of the people who paid it tribute in this ancient city. The flag floated purposelessly past the clock tower in the town square. A gust of wind swept the flag up and over yet another building. The breeze unfurled it long enough to provide a glimpse of the cross that guided its people for generations.

Petra opened her mouth and took in a deep breath, tasting the familiar salt in the air. It rested on her tongue and should have been a balm for her discouraged heart.

Ashes smudged the flag's blue background. Its white cross speckled with dried, rust-colored blood. The wind diminished, and the flag, slowly, started on an aimless downfall.

What of all the flags that flew in this cosmopolitan city, so many that claimed to have been allies to the Greeks? Damn them. A hundred curses on their black souls for leaving so many Greeks at the mercy of the Turks. So many and yet so few allies stepped forward to help the Greek citizens trapped in a land so beloved and yet so persecuting.

She watched the dilapidated Greek flag descend. She wanted to leap from the second story window and climb down the night jasmine trellis to save it before it touched the ground.

Petra held her breath as it reached the ornamental wrought iron barbs of the balcony next door. She prayed that the beloved symbol of her country would catch, for she could not leave this building to save it.

Stay aloft. Stay. As if this one flag could mirror the fate of an entire people — or even one family.

This piece previously appeared as part of another work by Stella Riley writing as Stella Sinclair. Stella was born in Greece and came to the US when she was fifteen years old. Her first novel is scheduled for publication in the summer.

Josephine Baker, *Et Tu Vivante*?
Based on Events in the Life of Dr. Doris Forté

Bob Collins

"I'm sorry," I said. "Did you say you were an optimist?"

"No," said Josephine. "An optometrist. I am an optometrist. There is a difference, you know."

"What's the difference?" I asked jokingly.

"Well," she said smiling, "it's a matter of a degree or two."

I first met Josephine not long ago on a Saturday morning at Barnes and Noble. You know the book sellers with the coffee shop. I was looking for some good fiction to read and as I turned into the aisle, I bumped into her.

"I'm so sorry," I said. "I didn't even see you." We looked at each other for a couple of seconds.

"I'm Josephine," she said. "Some people call me Josie, but I like Josephine better."

"I'm Roberto. By accident of birth. Apparently someone at the hospital added an 'o' to my name, and my parents didn't have enough money to get it changed. Most people call me Bob," I said as I extended my hand.

"I think I'll call you Roberto." She smiled, slightly raising her hands to show coffee in one and books in the other. "You can't see very well, can you Roberto?" Josephine asked.

"Why do you ask?" I was somewhat taken aback by her bookstore, three minute diagnosis.

"Well, isn't it obvious?" She asked. "You didn't look like you were lost in thought. In fact, you looked like you were in a hurry. And besides, no guy bumps into any woman from ten feet away unless they want to cop a feel."

"I was in a bit of a hurry. I went to the office this morning to finish a project and forgot to eat breakfast. I just wanted to stop in, get a book, and then get some lunch."

"Are you diabetic?" Josephine asked.

"Well," I hesitated, turning red, "yes I am."

"We need to get you over to the coffee shop and get some orange juice in you. You're starting to get shaky." she observed.

The last thing I remember was Josephine putting her books on the floor and gently taking a hold of my arm. Then I fell against her, my head hitting her breast and thinking how nice it felt as I drifted off and slid to the floor with Josephine's arms around me.

I felt wonderful when I woke up but didn't know where I was. I moved my eyes to the left and right and saw nothing but bookshelves. *This isn't my bedroom*, I thought to myself.

Then I saw Josephine. Her arms were outstretched, like Christ at the Crucifixion, naked from the waist up with only a bra on, and talking to a police officer like she was a two-year old.

"I'm only trying to help, officer," she said. "You can see I'm not carrying anything. You were searching so hard, I thought I'd take my shirt off and make it easier!"

"Josephine?" I asked.

"Sir, are you all right?" asked the police woman.

"What?" I replied.

"I said, 'sir, are you all right?'"

"Yes, I'm fine. Why do you ask?" I was confused.

"Because you fainted in the store," the policewoman said, "and someone called us." Turning to Josephine, the police woman said, "Put your shirt back on ma'am."

"I am only trying to help, officer," Josephine repeated.

"Put your shirt back on, ma'am. Or I'll arrest you for indecent exposure," the officer said.

As I watched Josephine put her shirt back on, the officer turned to me, "Do you need an ambulance?"

"No, I'm fine," I said.

"Are you sure?" she asked.

"Yes, officer. I'm diabetic and I fainted," I said.

"You need to get yourself checked out," the officer said as she walked away. I could hear her call on the walkie-talkie that the situation was resolved. She said it was another stupid citizen who didn't have the sense God gave him. I was offended, but then Josephine knelt down beside me.

"You're okay. But we need to get some lunch in you. And by the way mister," she said smiling, "Gimme my books back! That's my reading material for tonight!"

I lifted my head and she took her books. She helped me up, and we started walking out of the store as the crowd gawked.

"My car's at the office," I said.

"Where's your office?" Josephine asked.

"About five minutes from here," I said.

"Well, my car's over here. You're not walking or driving until I get some lunch in you, and I know just the place."

As we were driving to the restaurant, Josephine asked "By the way, you never told me what you did for a living. What is it that you do?"

"I'm an engineer," I said.

She started laughing.

"What's so funny about that?" I asked.

"Well, you're not going to be able to play with your erector set unless you take better care of yourself!" she said.

'Oh, aren't you the funny one," I replied. "What happened back there anyway?" I asked.

"What happened to you or what happened to me?" Josephine asked coyly.

"To both of us," I replied.

"Well, you fainted and I grabbed you, easing you to the ground. I slid my books under your head and got my Swiss Army knife out and someone from the crowd called the police saying I pulled a knife on you. I always carry around a Swiss Army knife. For emergencies, like yours."

"Like mine?" I asked.

"Yep. Like yours. I knew your blood sugar was low so I took out two honey packs from my purse and opened them with the scissors from my Swiss Army knife. I always open all the ketchup and mustard and honey packs with a scissors because whenever I tear them, they always spill out to the side. This way I can squeeze it out, and that's what I did for you."

"You did what?" I asked.

"Raised your head on my books, opened the honey packs and squeezed them under your tongue. I knew then it would take about fifteen minutes for you to start coming around"

"How did you know that?" I asked.

"Because I'm diabetic, too," Josephine said.

"Well, it's lucky I ran into you," I said thankfully.

"Yep. Literally as well as figuratively," she said. "Oh yeah, while you were out, I measured your blood sugar. I always carry my meter around with me.

That's about the time the police showed up. By the way, your blood sugar was way under the minimum. So I opened another honey pack and put it under your tongue. That's when the police officer grabbed me and pushed me against the book shelves."

"Why?" I asked.

"Because some hysterical lady called them and said I had a knife and was robbing you," Josephine said as she rolled her eyes.

"As she was frisking me, I sensed this officer was acting lesbianesque. She was feeling the outline of my bra and ran her hands down my ass in a much too friendly way. And I got pissed, took my shirt off, and told her she could search me better without any clothes on."

"What happened next?" I asked.

"The police woman and I knew what was going on, but the crowd didn't. I started thinking, *here I am with dreadlocks and a tattoo on my hand. If I don't defuse this, I might end up in jail.* That's when I apologized to the officer, and that's when you woke up, thank goodness."

"Why didn't you just wait for the police or the paramedics?" I asked.

"What do you think I am, stupid? I was raised on a farm where we had all kinds of emergencies. I knew you were diabetic, and I knew what you needed. The annoying thing about this was that the people in the crowd kept telling me to stop or they would call the police. And, so I guess that's why the police arrived and not the paramedics. Any more questions, mister engineer?"

"No, I guess not," I said as she parked her car in front of a house.

"Here we are! Chez Josephine," she said.

"I thought we were going to a restaurant?" I must have looked confused.

"I didn't say anything about a restaurant," she said. "I'm going to cook you a decent meal while you sit by the pool. Then afterwards I'm going to set up a case file on you. I want to give you an eye exam. If not today, then tomorrow.

"Tomorrow's Sunday," I replied.

"Yes, but you have an in with the doctor," she said smiling.

I was hungry.

After lunch, Josephine changed into a bathing suit top, jeans, and an open shirt. She came out with two glasses of iced tea in her hands and tucked into her bathing suit top were a couple of pens, a small pad of paper and her thumb drive.

"I'm giving you some sweet tea to raise your blood sugar levels," she said as she handed me the glass.

"Why do you carry so much in your top?" I asked.

"Because I only have two hands, mister engineer! Or didn't you notice that?" She rolled her eyes at me.

She put her iced tea down and began clearing the table, taking the lunch plates back into the kitchen. I felt sleepy. The weather was perfect, and the waterfall at the end of the pool sounded like a lullaby as I began to drift off.

"You're not going to sleep yet, mister," Josephine said. "I need to get some information from you for when I do your eye exam. Then, I can have a better feel for how bad your eyesight is."

She set up her computer on the table, inserted her thumb drive and began asking me all sorts of questions. It seemed to go on forever, and I was becoming annoyed.

"Is all this really necessary?" I asked.

"It is, if you want to get better," she shot back. "Besides I do my case files quickly, and I keep them all on my thumb drive so I can carry them with me all the time. Just a few more questions and we're almost done."

When we finished, she removed the thumb drive, put it safely back into her top and closed the computer.

"Do you want any more iced tea?" she asked as she got up.

"Yes, thanks."

As Josephine reached down to get my glass, the thumb drive fell out of her top and took one bounce into the pool.

Holy shit!" she yelled. "Hold these!" She handed me the glasses and jumped into the pool to retrieve the drive.

"Are you files gone?" I asked, knowing full well they were. Everyone knows what it is like to lose files accidentally, and this was one of the worst accidents I had seen.

"I haven't backed up these files in over a month!" she said. "If I don't do something, I'll lose all these case files and a month's work! Holy shit!"

"Is there anything I can do?" I asked helplessly.

"As a matter of fact, there is," she said as she sat back down, put the thumb drive on the table, and pulled out her Swiss Army knife. "Do you have a handkerchief?"

"Yes, but it's dirty," I said.

"I didn't ask for a clean handkerchief!" she snapped back at me as she gently opened the thumb drive with the edge of her knife. "I asked if you had a handkerchief!"

"Yes, I do," I said as I tried to hand it to her.

"I don't want it, you idiot!" she growled. "I want you to gently try to get the water out of the drive. Oxidation occurs immediately in these things, and if we don't act quickly, all the data will be lost. In fact, I'm not sure anything we do will help. Just gently dab the handkerchief on the drive and try to get all the water out while I run to the kitchen."

She raced back to the table with a box of wild rice and an empty jar.

"Did you do what I told you?" she talked to me as if I were an idiot.

"Yep," I said.

Josephine took a quick look. "Your eyesight is worse than I thought," she yelled at me. "Give me the handkerchief!" And she proceeded to gently remove all the water in the thumb drive.

"This was going to be part of my dinner, tonight," she said as she opened the wild rice and poured it into the jar. She then took both halves of the thumb drive and placed them on top of the rice and gently poured more rice over them, fully covering both pieces.

"We won't know for twenty-four hours if the data is okay," she said shoulders drooping. "I give it a fifty, fifty chance."

"I'm so very sorry," I said trying to provide comfort. "I know very well how bad it is to lose data."

"Well, mister engineer, we don't know if it is lost. We won't know that until tomorrow," she said.

"Maybe I should be going," I said.

"Yes, you should! But you don't have a car," she said. "But, I would like you gone, too! You've caused me enough trouble for one day. In the future, please don't go to that Barnes and Noble. That's my favorite place, and I don't like running into strangers like you!"

I felt bad but nothing I could do would help.

"Let me see your feet," she said.

"My feet?" I asked.

"Yes, your feet. Are you deaf? As long as you're here, I'll finish your exam," she said calmly.

Annoyed, I asked, "Why does an eye doctor need to see my feet?"

"Look, mister engineer. I'm not asking you to take your pants off, am I? Just take your shoes and socks off and let me see your feet. I'll bet the diabetes has made your feet numb."

"Yes they are, as a matter of fact. They've been that way for a long time."

"Well, let's check them out," she said as I took my shoes and socks off.

Josephine gasped. "How long has your foot been like this?"

"Like what?" I asked.

"Like this, asshole. You're not getting an eye exam tomorrow. You're going to the emergency room right now! You've got gas gangrene. Can't you feel it? Can't you smell it?"

"No, I thought my feet were fine," I said. "I try to check them out regularly."

"With your eyesight? You must be crazy. Why didn't you have someone else check them out? Like your wife or girlfriend or neighbor?"

"I'm not married, I don't have a girlfriend, and my neighbor and I haven't spoken in years. Are you sure it's gangrene?" I asked.

"You're an idiot child! I wrote all about this in my book *Combat Doctor: My Life in the 1st Air Cavalry*."

"I saw a movie by the same name. Is that you?" I asked incredulously. "But I don't remember anything about gangrene in the movie."

"Did you read the fucking book, or not?" she demanded.

"No, I didn't read the fucking book!" I retorted. "I only saw the movie. It reminded me of Flashman's *Dawns and Departures*. But that was fiction."

"Well, mine wasn't!" she said. "Now get your ass up. We're going to the emergency room! If we don't go now, you'll lose your leg in a day or so and then your life."

So, with one foot in the grave, we left for the nearest E.R. Dr. Josephine Baker saved my life *and* the data on her thumb drive. Out of gratitude, I switched to another Barnes and Noble.

Bob Collins is an ex-buffalo hunter from South Texas and writes after his work is done for the day. In the evening he enjoys a good cigar when he can afford it and Budweiser beer. Trust me, he can afford both at the same time.

Other Works by Members of the Houston Writers Guild

Ghosts, Strange Tales of the Unnatural, the Uncanny and the Unaccountable
Edited by Lynne Gregg and Julian Kindred
Aakenbaaken & Kent, ISBN: 978-1-938436-07-9

Is there a ghost in your life? Do you see people that aren't there? We warn you, don't read these tales when you are home alone. Stories by writers who understand where and when ghosts may bring good or evil to your daily routine. Or sometimes, just a laugh.

Bought Off
by Roger Paulding
Aakenbaaken & Kent, ISBN: 978-1-938436-09-3

Suave, buttoned-down Alex Upchurch seems an odd match with his position as Assistant District Attorney of Galveston, a city some say is like the antique store on the north end that advertises "Mostly Junque, a Few Jewels." But when a dead John Doe is discovered naked in the bedroom of Alex's baronial mansion, District Attorney John Henry Davenport has to cover up the crime to save not only his able assistant but also to placate Alex's Mother, Honey Upchurch, whose money bought John Henry's position. Figuring out who is dead and why proves almost as challenging as keeping that information from becoming known, especially when Alex is appointed to prosecute a former lover who knows all but tells nothing. Fortunately, Leon McAdoo, known as Miss Starlight because of a gossip column he (or she?) writes, is on hand to guide us through the maze of power, money, sex and corruption.

The Pot Thief Who Studied Billy the Kid
by J. Michael Orenduff
The 6th and latest book in this wildly-popular and award winning series
Aakenbaaken & Kent, ISBN: 978-1-938436-06-2

While illegally digging for Anasazi pots in a cliff dwelling, Hubert Schuze grasps a human hand. He was hoping for an artifact, not a handshake and is puzzled by his discovery. The Anasazi did not bury their dead in their living quarters. A more pressing problem confronts him when he hears his truck drive away from the plain above the cliff. The rope he was planning to use to return to the surface was attached to the truck's winch. After a bizarre escape from the cliff dwelling, he is convinced to return by his sidekick Susannah who suspects the body was not a mummy but a contemporary person. But when Hubie descends a second time with her help, what he discovers defies all logic. It takes Hubie, Susannah, a coyote and Billy the Kid to finally figure out who was dead and why.

The Pot Thief Who Studied Pythagoras
by J. Michael Orenduff
The book that started it all. Winner (Kindle version), 2010 "Eppie" as best e-book mystery of the year
Aakenbaaken & Kent, ISBN: 978-1-938436-00-0

When a shady character offers him $25,000 to steal a thousand-year-old pot from the Valle del Rio Museum, Hubert Schuze knows he should turn it down. His pot digging may be illegal, but it's a big step from that to robbery. But he figures it can't hurt just to visit the museum and assay his chances. He figured wrong. After deciding the museum is impregnable, he returns to his shop to find a BLM agent who accuses him of stealing the rare pot. Theft charges escalate to murder. Hubert's powerful deductive skills and weak nerves are put to the test as he solves the crime and clear himself.

The Pot Thief Who Studied Einstein
by J. Michael Orenduff
The 3rd book in the series and winner of the 2011 LEFTY AWARD for best humorous mystery novel of the year
Aakenbaaken & Kent, ISBN: 978-1938436-02-4

Maybe it was the chance for an easy $2500. Or maybe it was the chance to examine a treasure trove of Anasazi pots. Or maybe it was just a slow day at his Old Town Albuquerque shop that enticed Hubie Schuze to be blindfolded and chauffeured to meet a reclusive collector looking for a confidential appraisal. Sure, it was an odd setup, but what could possibly go wrong? Hubie s devil-may-care attitude fades fast when he finds three of his own Anasazi copies among the genuine antiquities. Worse, when the driver drops him back home, what he doesn't find are the twenty-five crisp hundred dollar bills the collector paid him. Hubie is determined to recoup his cash, but Detective Whit Fletcher interrupts, dragging Hubie to the morgue to identify a John Doe. When the sheet is pulled back, Hubie is stunned to see the collector. Hubie is not a suspect yet. But the longer he pursues his missing appraisal fee, the more tangled he becomes in the collector's shadowy life.

The Pot Thief Who Studied D. H. Lawrence
by J. Michael Orenduff
The 5th book in the series
Aakenbaaken & Kent, ISBN: 978-1938436-04-8

D. H. Lawrence wrote of the winter on Taos Mountain, "In a cold like this, the stars snap like distant coyotes." Hubie's official reason for visiting the Lawrence Ranch high on that Mountain is to entertain donors with a presentation about ancient pottery. But his real goal is to find the pot Fidelio Duran presented to D. H. Lawrence as a welcoming gift. Then a snowstorm strands Hubie at the Lawrence Ranch Conference Center, and his new goal becomes survival. Are the guests dying of accidents or is there a murderer among them?

The Pot Thief Who Studied Escoffier
by J. Michael Orenduff
The 4th book in the series
Aakenbaaken & Kent, ISBN: 978-1938436-03-1

Old Town Albuquerque potter Hubie Schuze agrees to create unique chargers for the table settings in a soon-to-open Austrian restaurant in Santa Fe. Once onsite, Hubie is immersed in the politics of the restaurant business. In an effort to negotiate the egos and agendas, Hubie invites the *grillardin* for cocktails. The inebriated grill cook insists on snoozing in Hubie's truck, but the next morning,

Hubie finds the *garde manger* there instead... not breathing and as cold as his menu items. Before Hubie can recover from the shock, things spiral out of control at *Schnitzel*, forcing the eatery to close its doors. Unwilling to cede defeat, the kitchen staff convince Hubie to help them convert to a Mexican-Austrian fusion menu. The reviews are rave and the money rolls in, but Hubie is soon faced with that old prophecy — no good deed goes unpunished.

The Pot Thief Who Studied Ptolemy
by J. Michael Orenduff
The 2nd book in the series
Aakenbaaken & Kent, ISBN: 978-1938436-01-7

The pot thief is back, but this time Hubert Schuze' larceny is for a good cause. He wants to recover sacred pots stolen from San Roque, the mysterious New Mexico pueblo closed to outsiders. An easy task for Hubert Schuze, pot digger. Except these pots are not under the ground— they're 150 feet above it. In the top-floor apartment of Rio Grande Lofts, a high-security building which just happens to be one story above Susannah's latest love interest. Hubie's legendary deductive skills lead to a perfect plan which is thwarted when he encounters the beautiful Stella. And when he is arrested for murder. Well, he was in the room where the body was found, everyone heard the shot, and he came out with blood on his hands. Follow Hubie as he stays one step ahead of building security, one step behind Stella, and one step away from a long fall down a garbage chute.

The Pickled Dog Caper Crime – Murder and Mayhem in Colonial Days
by Roger Paulding
Forthcoming from Aakenbaaken & Kent in 2013

CPSIA information can be obtained at www.ICGtesting.com
Printed in the USA
LVOW060616010413

326929LV00001B/89/P